Journey Home

First Edition

Published by The Nazca Plains Corporation
Las Vegas, Nevada
2008

ISBN: 978-1-934625-89-7

Published by

The Nazca Plains Corporation®
4640 Paradise Rd, Suite 141
Las Vegas NV 89109-8000

PUBLISHER'S NOTE
Journey Home is a work of fiction created wholly by *Theivandran's*
imagination. All characters are fictional and any resemblance to any persons
living or deceased is purely by accident. No portion of this book reflects
any real person or events.

Cover, Blake Stephens
Art Director, Blake Stephens

Journey Home

First Edition

Theivandran

Table of Contents

Chapter 1 ......

*Now in the present. Arriving at
Colombo Sri Lanka Airport*

Kumar, woke from his half dazed sleep as Air Lanka circled the airport to get permission to land in Sri Lanka As he rubbed his eyes and peeped out he saw the green coconut palm trees sway in the Island breeze, and small colorfully dressed brown people scurrying around. Why he questioned himself he was walking back into a childhood nightmare. For the last 40 years his sleep had been disturbed with the persisting night mare of something so bitter sweet, yet incomprehensible for him or his physiatrist. Now he felt as he was walking into the nightmare with eyes wide open. Things in USA had moved so fast that he could not believe that he was just looking at the dawn breaking in his peaceful back yard nursing a cup of coffee and mediating to his God just 48 hours ago.

The shrill of his telephone and the bitter sobbing of his youngest sister-in-law pierced his peaceful morning. Padmini was his youngest brother's wife and was pregnant with her third child. His youngest brother Alfred grew in Kumar's home and completed his medical degree and is practicing in California a few miles from Kumar's residence. Kumar had smuggled his mother and baby brother to this country to escape his father's abuse and the unrest that was growing between the races that lived in Sri Lanka. Kumar had witnesses the racial riots and bloodshed that destroyed the peace of the Island in 1958. Kumar's maternal grandfather, in whose ranch his mother and 4 brothers found sanctuary knew and groomed Kumar to venture out of the country and open doors for that extended family to escape the brutality of racial cleansing. Kumar had kept his promise to his grandfather. The whole family had migrated to the USA, before the Tamils formed a terrorist group to destroy everything beautiful that existed in that peaceful island.

As Kumar exited the plane, a warm island breeze seem to kiss him a long lost welcome kiss. How could such a beautiful peaceful island which legend has pointed out that God even placed the Garden of Eden in this part of the world go so violent. From his childhood Kumar had witnessed man's cruelty to each other starting from his own father and the others around him. This was one reason Kumar had built such a wall around his heart and stayed as a recluse in his home in the USA. He never wanted to revisit this part of the world or relive his dark and uncomprehendable nightmare. Now he was walking right into it. Yet fear was not in his veins and there seem to be certain calmness in his whole demeanor.

A few months ago the terrible tsunami and destroyed many parts of this island and the natives were left with no medical help. Alfred had volunteered to take medicines and help a certain orphanage in the east coast of Sri Lanka. The family had tried to persuaded him that this mission was to dangerous for a young man who had no clue of the culture or language of the country to venture into the jungle on such a mission. The USA government too informed them that this area is under terrorist control. Alfred felt that it was his duty and God given responsibility to help his mother land. Although Kumar was secretly proud and happy to see the boy that he raised in this new and strange land, with a completely new language and culture still hold on to the love of his mother land, fear did keep him up many nights. Kumar knew that there will be dangers all around a western grown and educated young man. Finally through net working, Kumar was able to trace a friend of the family and pleaded with him to act as Alfred's companion in this mission. Selvarajah happily agreed as he knew Alfred as a baby and wanted to see how this home town boy had grown into such a man. So the group traveled in to the jungles and set up a make shift medical clinic to help the natives. Selvarajah telephoned Kumar daily to give the report of the progress, and things seem to move smoothly. The news of a doctor with free medicines spread like wild fire. Crowds started to approach the clinic in hundreds. Alfred did not stop from early morning till sometimes mid night treating patients. Selvarajah was worried that these long hours of work and no proper nutrient will break Alfred down. Then suddenly the phone calls did not come, third morning Kumar finds out that his sister in law Padmini had a brief telephone call from Alfred stating that he and Selvarajah had been kidnapped by the Tamil Tigers. The terrorist had taken them from the camp into the deep jungles to help their injured. Since the medicines had all been given out, Alfred had made a deal with the captors to let him go back to the USA, and collect more medicines and return, but the terrorist needed some one to be the hostage in Alfred's place, Selvarajah had volunteered but they turned down his offer as the terrorists felt he had no influence on Alfred's promise. The terrorist wanted Padmini to come and take her husband's place. She was 7 months pregnant and had two little boys to take care, thus the lot to be a pawn in this game became Kumar's lot. Kumar was a 63 years old retired teacher, had an incurable disease and most of all alone in this world. So Kumar volunteered to take his baby brother's place in the terrorist's hideaway till Alfred returned with a new supply of medicines. So here Kumar is slowly dragging himself out of the airplane to rescue his baby bother. While standing on line to go through customs and immigration, he notices all the army men and women with guns scurrying like ants around the whole compound. The tigers had bombed a part of the airport a few days before. According to the TV news they had purchased parts of a plane, from a western country, assembled it in the jungle hideaway and flown it to the main airport in Colombo and destroyed a part of it. Kumar wondered why he was again the rescuer for his family. Why he could not live his last days in peace with out the strange recurring nightmare which was strangely connected to this part of the world. The country which was once known as God's Garden of Eden. Why did fate curse him to be born here and may be fate has brought him back to die here. Death at this point did not seem to matter, getting Alfred out was the only goal that seemed to haunt Kumar's heart, but was there a bigger picture than this one man's escape.

Chapter 2 ......

The Airport incidents at Sri Lanka

Kumar walked through the customs and immigration as if they were expecting him, his lack of luggage or the only nap sac on his back did not seem to cause any suspicion. He walked towards the bank window and cashed two of his $100.00 traveler's checks and was surprised at the exchange rate. The Sri Lankan currency seems to be so week compared to the American dollars. How could people survive this way Kumar thought to himself? As he found the exit that was in the far end and walked out into the morning sun, which blinded him. It has been ages since Kumar wore a watch, but just surmised it was around 7 Am. Now he tried to find a flower vender as they had instructed him. Then he saw the old woman with a small push cart with brightly colored native flowers. He was instructed to buy one red Anthuriam, a flower grown in the hills, in the remote areas of the country. Kumar could not believe his eyes; the old woman did not have one red flower in her cart, not even a red carnation which grew in abundance in this part of the world. The old wrinkled woman grinned at him, trying to sell him some of her wares. Her face was beaten down by the harsh sun and was like a wrinkled prune. Kumar thought it would crack into a million pieces if she grinned any more. She had lost most of a teeth, may be due to chewing tobacco and beetle leaves to kill the hunger due to her poor lot in this country. Her eyes stood out, they were deep pools of muddy yet compassionate reflection of peace. Kumar after 40 years had forgotten the language and was trying to inquire in English if she had a red flower, the woman looked puzzled. She kept giving Kumar a pleading look to buy some of her beautiful yellow orchids. Finally looking all over Kumar found a red dot on his boarding pass and showed it to her, and she grinned and pulled a small bucket of red Anthuriams she had hidden under her cart. Strange Kumar thought every one would have bought theses, but she kept it hidden till he had pointed and asked for red flower. Kumar took 10 rupees and gave it to her. Her old shriveled fingers grabbed the note and she picked a bunch of theses beautiful, elegant flowers and wrapped them, in an old newspaper very gently, but Kumar reached and pulled just one, bowed and walked looking for a bus stop under a big shady tree as he was instructed to do. The woman grinned, picked a cart and rolled it towards the main entrance of the airport.

Chapter 3 ......

The journey begins... reflections of youth

Kumar found the bus stop further away, but near the army check point. There was an army check point that stopped every vehicle that entered the driveway of the airport. The soldiers seemed to be courteous but there was lots of commotion as passengers or drivers did not seem to like this delay. Kumar was far enough that he could not understand or comprehend the sometimes, heated conversations. Kumar pulled out his bottle of water and took a sip thinking how long this water and his waiting is going to last. He was getting hungry and wished that he had the common sense to eat before coming out. The crowd at the bus stop was thinning, and the buses were rolling off. Dust and smoke rose like big storm clouds, so Kumar moved a little away to sit under huge Banyan tree that had a few stone benches underneath its huge shade. The leaves and the supportive roots formed a natural temple. As Kumar sat there his mind took him back to his childhood.

He remembered the huge tree that formed a cave like appearance in his home town. In the early sixties, Tamils from that part had started to protest against the Singhalese run government. The Tamils felt that their children were not treated fairly by the government of Sri Lanka. There were no chances for Tamil teens to get a higher education, as the government prohibited them, to enter the one university in Sri Lanka. So they started civil disobedience following in the foot steps of Mahatma Gandhi. A nonviolent protest to sabotage the working of the government offices. Men and women sat in front of government offices day and night singing prayers and blocking any one entering or leaving theses offices. Finally after a few months the government sent the army to disperse the crowd. Around 2 am, the army matched in and beat and dispersed most of the protesters. Kumar, who also was a Tamil, was on the site running the first aid stand for the protestors. The boys scouts of the near by schools took turns manning this stand and as Kumar lived near that area, he was called to do the mid night shift. Kumar loved this type of adventure, but knew his grandfather was there too, His grandfather supervised the civil disobedience during this part of the night, so the leaders could rest and come in the day time to take over. As the soldiers approached and dispersed the crowd who kept calling on the various Gods to help them, Kumar stood frozen at his stand. Then he saw this young solider, approach him and point to his hand. Kumar noticed that the man had been cut, and was bleeding. Being a gentle boy, Kumar made him sit and dressed his wound. While he was dressing the wound, the young solider, very gently slipped his good hand into Kumar's trousers. Kumar felt an instant hard on, that made him blush and as the man touched his penis, Kumar shot his load. This was his first orgasm, unable explain this event, and the thrill of the moment, Kumar felt a deep attraction to this enemy solider. The young man, rubbed Kumar's wet gummy penis, and in broken English told Kumar to meet the next day at the Jaffna beach near the entrance of the Jaffna fort. So started Kumar's homosexual encounter with the enemy solider. Like clock work Kumar would meet this man and they would masturbate each other. As time went by more men would come to the spot and get Kumar to play with their full grown penises. Kumar too loved to feel the pubic hair, the heavy large nuts and the throbbing hard shafts of theses men, and watch them spew their seed. They would feel Kumar's hairless thighs and get turned on. There was no other play but just sheer masturbation. As Kumar was recollecting theses child hood memories and watching the young army men scurrying around, he thought to him self how much more I can teach theses guys now, and smiled to himself.

Chapter 4 ……

Blessing from Lord Buddha

Suddenly out of no where he heard this voice. "Good morning, my young man" The accent was heavy yet the voice was deep. Kumar looked around and behind sat an old gentle man in a clean sarong and a white yet wet tee shirt, wet due to his sweat from the humid air. Kumar returned the greetings. The old gentle man had a small bottle of white liquid that looked like milk, and a small saucer. "I have come to feed Lord Buddha", he commented as he poured the milk into the saucer and very gingerly moved towards the trunk of the huge tree. The old man placed it at a point where there was a huge hole in the bark. It looked like a small but yet prominent cave. Then he backed off very calmly and sat next to Kumar. He seemed to saying something under his breath. It sounded like a chant. Kumar was afraid to ask him any thing as the man seemed to be mesmerized in his devotion. Suddenly a huge Cobra slithered out of the cave and started to drink the milk. The color of this snake was light grey. Both men sat in complete silence and waited for the snake to finish his meal in peace. The old snake sipped the milk very calmly taking it's time to enjoy his meal. After completing his meal, the Cobra raised its hood surveyed the area, froze for few minutes and retrieved into his abode. The man turned to Kumar and in a very soft tone said, "My son, you have Lord Buddha's blessing in your quest to find peace, go with out fear. I have come here for many years hoping to see this legend, but only today the reincarnation of the Lord Buddha showed himself to us. This is a good omen and a blessing that the universe is behind you. Your journey has been a long one, and till you rectify your errors, your soul will be restless and wondered through many lives to correct its errors. You are almost at your end of the quest, go without fear". He got up and walked away with out looking back, leaving Kumar in total amazement. Only then did Kumar realize why this tree and its surrounding seem so peaceful in the midst of the entire hullabaloo. It would have been a strange sight for passersby to see a brown man, in western garb, holding one red flower and sitting under this huge tree alone. Kumar wondered if the world looked at Lord Buddha the same way when he mediated and found the path to nirvana. Although a strange sense of peace ran through Kumar's whole body, he felt more confused at the strangers' remark. What errors? What did I do to cause so much wondering and suffering? Is my lifestyle really a God given curse? How can the Lord create me and then punish me for his error. Every negative remark that was drilled into his head as a boy about his desire for the same sex flooded his head. So even death will not release me of this error? Kumar felt dejected, but reminded himself of his immediate goal of rescuing his baby brother, and try to pull himself out the path of the clouds of depression that darkened his soul. Is my lifestyle and my nightmares connected? So many questions, and yet there are no answers. When will I find answers?

Chapter 5 ......

Getting ready for the adventure.

Kumar's whole body and mind seemed to be reeling in a daze, the long flight, the lack of proper food, and sleep did not help. Add to this Kumar did not even carry his blood pressure or HIV medications. He never left his home in California with out theses all theses years. Now he seems to feel that he had acted a little foolishly and walked away from all his beloved possessions with out a second thought. Out of nowhere there appeared a taxi. An old Morris Minor car which seems to make such a racket that could wake the dead. Kumar looked at the car as the dust settled. The driver was holding a red Anthuriam, and kept motioning him to approach the taxi. Slowly and hesitantly Kumar walked to the taxi. "I am your driver, sir" shouted the man, "get in please and quickly". Kumar jumped into the back seat like someone lifted and threw him in there. "Good morning, sir, my name is Simon, and I will take you to your rest house now". With out waiting for a response the man pressed the accelerator and the taxi roared and took off like a tiger in a hunt. Coming from the USA after so many years the status of the interior or the sound of the engine, did not make Kumar feel very comfortable, but the rosary and a small picture of the Madonna hanging on the rear view mirror, at least sent a kind of peace through Kumar's soul. He silently repeated the Lord's Prayer. This was the first morning in his adult life that he did not start his day with daily meditation. As a boy, he watched his grandmother a devoted Christian start her mornings with meditation. Kumar started to copy her throughout his college years until today.

The taxi left the main road to the city, and took a little less traveled dirt road, Kumar closed his eyes and decided to face what ever came up. Suddenly the taxi stopped in front of a quaint little bungalow with a beautifully well kept garden. "Sir", said Simon, "you will rest here for a few hours before we proceed" and pointed to the little gate. Kumar got out of the taxi and walked to the door, which opened and there stood a well dressed middle aged woman with her hands clasped in a greeting. "Namaste" she said and lead Kumar in. "You room is here and a bath is ready, I will have your clothes washed and pressed, there is a sarong on the bed. And a barber is waiting to give you a shave and haircut." She pointed to a door and walked away. A shave, Kumar, thought he has been sporting his beard for so many years. Strange in the USA, they wanted him to grow a beard so he will look older than his students; here they want him to look younger. Go with the flow he said to himself and entered the room stripped himself put on the beautiful black sarong and walked into the garden to meet this so called barber. The barber was a little stocky man with a pot belly and was sharpening his razor on a piece leather strip. The strip of worn out leather remind Kumar of his play room in his home and the strips he used to tie his sex partners with. He pointed a little stool for Kumar to sit and went to work without a word. In the USA, Kumar would look for hairdressers who were cute boys, flirt by placing his hands so to gently touch the men's crotches. Here he had no desire to even look at the man. The barber lathered Kumar's face with soapsuds and went to work, removing every bit of hair on his chin and face. Then he cleaned it with a moist towel and patted Kumar's shoulder to signify he was done. "Oh!" Exclaimed Kumar, "I left my wallet in the room, wait here for your money". And Kumar rushed in, but found his clothes gone but wallet sitting on the small dresser. Taking a few rupees he retuned to the garden and the man was gone. Stranger he thought to himself, but walked back in and entered the small bathroom and got busy with his bath. When he came out of the bathroom feeling like a new man, there was a tray of sweet smelling Sri Lankan Breakfast waiting for him. It had been so many years that he had tasted or even smelled the aroma of such food. His stomach just could not wait to taste this delicious food. Stringhoppers and a soup made out of coconut milk, just hit the spot. After devouring the food, Kumar crawled under the covers of this small twin bed, to catch a few winks. Life seem to take such a strange turn, a man who planned and executed every move of his and his family's life, now seem to be in the hands of the strangers. As he dozed off, he remembered the statement of Blanche from the play "A Street Car Named Desire". "I have always relied on the kindness of strangers".

Then he started his reoccurring nightmare, running through a dark cave looking for a way out. Kumar's nap was cut short by a loud knock on the door. Simon stood there with his clothes washed and pressed. "Get dressed sir, we have to leave in a few minutes" he commanded and vanished. As Kumar slipped on his underwear and jeans he realized they were washed and ironed. Kumar started to wear blue jeans so it would save him time and energy not to iron them. He slipped on his clothes, threw a few rupees on the bed, and walked out. The lady of the house was out by the main door talking to Simon in Singhalese. Kumar did not understand the conversation but the tone was pleasant. Kumar approached the lady and asked her how much he owed her. She broke into a big smile and said that it has been all taken care off. She bade them goodbye and scurried into the home and shut the door. As Kumar entered the cab, he inquired if there was a bank nearby so he could cash some more checks to pay the taxi fare. Simon smiled broadly and said that it has been all taken care of too. Although Kumar wanted to question him about who and where he decided to go with the flow and settled back in the seat and closed his eyes.

Chapter 6 ......

The journey home... a step closer?

As the sun hit the back of his head, and the taxi wound its way to the main road, Kumar knew they were traveling east, to where the Tigers were holding his brother hostage. Then the car suddenly came to a stop in a little tea shop, which seemed to be closed for business. The driver jumped out and ran behind the shack, leaving the taxi engine was still purring. There we go, Kumar told himself, all this sham had to come to an end, I am lost in this God forsaken country in some remote part, here I am trusting the rebels and following their instructions in blind faith. Kumar pulled himself out of the taxi. As Kumar stretched his worn out body to take a good look of the surrounding the driver was scurrying back to the car with a small basket, a pillow and an old rolled blanket. "Sir please get in, we need to leave, I did not want to wake you, but did stop to get you some fruits, hot tea and this to make it a little more comfortable in the back, we will be taking the side roads as the main roads have many army check points and we have to be at your destination at a certain time" the driver spit out the words without even looking at Kumar. Leaning and placing the basket on the floor of the back seat and throwing the pillow and blanket on the seat. At that point Kumar noticed the firm round ass this young man, and all his sexual desires that seem to be dead for the last week or so seem to erupt like a volcano. The boy's legs were hairless. Kumar seemed to get turned on men who were hairless and many of the men he sexually seduced were hairless white men. "Sir, there is fruits and tea in the thermos, relax, it is a long ride and it will be a long night for you, may I play some Sinhala tape music" asked the driver. "Sure" Kumar answered, and peeped inside the basket which held an old thermos, two mangos, a bunch of sweet bananas, a bunch of brightly colored Rambotans and few mangoostens. All fruits were grown in Sri Lanka. Kumar felt a little shamed of his thoughts. Now days of internet dating, many of Kumar's sex dates only have contact with him online and come to his home like sacrificial lambs not knowing what to expect. Kumar too is in the same boat but has the upper hand on the role he plays sexually. Kumar is what they classify as a dominant top and runs the show. Kumar inquires and finds out, what type of food, drink or music theses men like and has the stage set to seduce them sexually. In a strange way, this young driver seems to be doing that. Are we Sri Lankan people all like that, Kumar wondered? Are we so much gentler and romantic that the outside world takes us for weaklings? Is our hospitable nature misunderstood?

The original inhabitants of Sri Lanka were called Vedas, a primitive sort of humans. They were supposed to look like part animals and part humans. Ugly humans according to the then civilized world. Many thousands of years ago, a North Indian king had a son Vijay, who with his 100 friends plundered and terrorist his father's citizens. Unable to control his son or his friends the father captured his prince and his gang, put then on a boat with no roars and let them drift in the Indian Ocean. For days these men drifted, were sun parched, sick and hungry. Their boat ran ashore on a Sri Lankan beach and these handsome men were tended and cared for by the Vedas. When they got stronger and realized the tenderness of the Vedas, Vijay seduced the Veda leader's daughter and took power over the tribe then killed his wife and imported pretty dainty women from India to become their wives and queens. Thus kindness has been repaid by brutality in this countries history. The Portuguese, the Dutch, the French and the English had captured and poured poison into the hearts of the natives. So here we are today destroying each other. Yet this young man has gone out of his way to show Kumar the love in his heart. The driver slide in a tape and the singer started in his raspy and deep voice to say "the journey home is a never to long".

Chapter 7 ......

Welcome dance of Mother Nature...

As the taxi wound it's way into the side streets, going away from the main roads, Kumar tried to close his eyes and search for sleep, but the scenes outside, the gentle breeze, the aroma of mother natures perfume kept him wide awake like a small child in a toy store. He never entered to a toy store till he was an adult in USA, in those days there were no stores in Sri Lanka to sell toys. We boys found our fun in Mother Nature's lap. The brown skin men and women singing as they bend and weed their rice fields, the young boy trying herd a host of huge buffaloes, animals 6 to 7 times as big as himself, lazily claiming the narrow road as their territory, the tiny taxi trying to squeeze between them, and the sheepish look of annoyance from the huge buffaloes, the field hands making sure they do not enter into field, the quacking of the ducks, the screeching of the hens, the barking of dogs all made a sort of magical music. In his heart Kumar felt a warm feeling of belonging, although he knew deep within himself he was considered an outcaste not because of his family heritage but because of his innate desire for men. Then he remembered how man, changed all of Mother Nature's plans. The Sri Lankan natives knew how to terrace their hilly land and grow their staple diet, rice. Then came the white man with his so called education and wisdom and changed the whole way of life. Since the climate was conducive to grow tea, all the rice fields were demolished and tea plantations popped up. Rice was imported from another country which too was under British rule. Sri Lanka was renamed "Ceylon". Ceylon tea became the brew of the white world and money poured in to Sri Lanka. When the natives wanted the British give them independence and let them rule their country. They did leave, but also sabotaged the tea trade. So the natives had tea to drink by the gallons but no rice to stamp off their hunger. This was the beginning of ugly head of hatred waking up and destroying the land. Kumar noticed men and women brightly dressed in sarongs or saris, walking ahead and suspiciously looking at the approaching taxi, and unceremoniously moving out of its path. How we humans have adapted to fear, unlike the herd of buffalos who still claimed their right to this land. "It is market day, Sir" whispered the driver, as Kumar was still gazing at the dance of Mother Nature. Man can never keep her down, Kumar thought to himself, and proudly acclaimed he is in his own mother's arms. Kumar silently said a prayer of thanksgiving for her home coming party. He reflected the story of the prodigal son's return. Kumar had run so far but how far, can you run or hide from yourself. Kumar's eyes clouded with tears as he remembered the early days of childhood, when he ran and played bare foot and scantly dressed with his brothers. As Kumar looked up, he noticed the driver looking at him through the rear view mirror. There seem to be something different about him, Kumar thought, but just shrugged the feeling. Kumar turned his gaze to the welcome mat mother nature was rolling, as they drove over a small bridge, Kumar noticed the elephant herders bathing their huge yet lovable and extremely loyal animals in shallow stream, to cool them off in the mid day sun. The elephants were spraying each other and their masters with a mist of water. The world seemed not to have care in its heart, yet there was a strange heaviness in Kumar's soul. Kumar came back from his day dreaming when he heard the driver addressing him "Sir, Sir"

"There is an old man walking ahead with a small bag sir, seems to be a man of God, can I give him a ride" he asked almost pleading. "Sure" said Kumar as he tried to focus on the old man ahead. The old man was dressed in a faded, yet off colored white cassock, unkept grey beard and balding, grey head. In USA, we are warned to not to pick up hitchhikers or strangers, here every one is treated, like angels, Kumar thought to himself. The taxi came to grinding stop a few feet in front of the stranger and the driver leaned over, opening the door asked the man, if he wanted a ride. The stranger was in the taxi, next to the driver almost in a flash. They exchanged greeting and the taxi started on its way.

Chapter 8 ......

The strange hitchhiker in the forest.

The old man, turned to Kumar and smiled, his sun beaten face, blood shot eyes and rugged look was a testimony to his hard journey in life. Kumar noticed his black collar, and assumed he was a Christian priest. "Good morning, my boy" he addressed Kumar, "coming home?" Kumar just smiled at this old man. It has been too many years to count being called a boy, now it was Kumar who called his sex partners "boys" as he pierced their tight ass with his hard on, and they squirmed with a little pain mingled with sheer ecstasy. Also the thought of not checking himself in the mirror after the morning ritual shave popped in his mind. Kumar decided to just nod, bent and picked up the thermos and passed it to the stranger. "Sir, here is some tea; you can share it with the driver". Kumar sat back. The old man opened the bottle and poured some warm aromatic tea, passed it to the driver and started to sip from the bottle very gingerly and enjoy his tea. The aroma filled the taxi. Suddenly Kumar remembered once before strangers had mistook him not as a boy but as the youngest in his family of four brothers. It was in Atlanta, by his father's grave site. Kumar was in his forties diagnosed with the HIV virus and given a few months to live. As this was a new disease and people believed it was God's curse on homosexuals, and teachers with this disease was been laid off Kumar had decided to move to California to find a new lease in life, once before visiting the Coachella valley, Kumar found that the American Indian's regarded the valley as the hollow of God's palm. So Kumar had somehow made his way to live in this scared part of the world. But before leaving the old stumping grounds he had brought his father from the remote part of Georgia to live close to him in Atlanta. That year somehow father and son made peace, Kumar accepted his father's short comings of being a parent and the father accepted his son's sexual desire and life style. Almost at end of Kumar's stay in that part of the world, his father passed away. And here they were all 4 brothers burying and saying good bye to their father. One of the strangers, who stopped by to mourn with the family mistook Kumar to be the youngest in the family, and was surprised when corrected. That night at the dinner table Kumar's mother in her gentle demeanor recalled her romance with her husband. Looking at Kumar she said in a sure voice, that never forgets my son, you were conceived in love, and you are a love child that is why there is such a glow in your soul. The past memories seem to flood Kumar's brain and clash likes waves at high tide.

Then suddenly the strange old hitchhiker started to mumble in an audible, yet bitter tone, "Some of us are searching all our lives to find the meaning of our existence, we walk this life looking for a meaning, why and where, some feel wealth and others feel knowledge will set them free, I know there is a purpose for all of us, I am in my nineties, yet I seem lost but you young boy seem to be so close to your purpose and desire, I do envy you. Maybe my lot in life is to point you in the right direction. The Lord has been kind and loving to you to give you so many chances to succeed in your mission, even death could not defeat you, nor distance or time in accomplishing your mission. Remember, it is the unhappy and fearful humans who try to change the nature's law. You should clear your mind of all the trash that has been forced into you. The Lord of this universe is an extremely kind and loving parent, He never leads any one astray. You my boy may feel confused and dejected, but there is help for you all around. When the student is ready the teacher will appear. " He kept on rambling and Kumar first was uncertain whom he was addressing till he realized the priest was addressing him and not the driver, who was lost in his own world of maneuvering the car through the maze of people in the tiny village. If the Lord in this old man's belief is extremely kind, why are homosexuals banned from worshiping in certain churches? Kumar wanted to ask this priest but decided that keeping quiet would be the proper thing to do. "Ha!" pointed his bony finger towards a tiny procession of people claded in white attire, carrying a small pyre walking solemnly into secluded part of the end of the village. The driver brought the taxi to sudden halt, out of respect to the dead and mourning. The priest continued "that is sure one lucky soul, no more searching, only joy waiting in paradise. We on the other hand will drag on to find our destiny, who knows how and when." Kumar did feel for this poor soul, but as he watched the procession he noticed a young woman with three children clinging to her and walking behind the corpse. Suddenly tears welled and overflowed from Kumar's eyes, misting his glasses. He remembered a story his grand father had told him, many moons ago. Kumar must have been just twelve years old, when a beggar had approached his grandfather's ranch pleading for a slice of bread. His grandfather had invited this man in, allowed him to bath at the well, given him clean cloths to wear and fed him and put some money in his hand as he bade him good bye. This action did astound Kumar as there were many beggars in that part of the world. "Papa, Kumar approached his grandfather, "why special treatment for this beggar?"

The story his grandfather told him resurfaced now in Kumar's heart. When his grandfather was only five years old his father died, his step brother who was raised as one of the sons by his mother had just turned eighteen, and was given the responsibility of caring for the family. No sooner than the corpse was removed from the home to be burned on the pyre, this young man threw his young illiterate step mother and her three boys on the street. The mother had to do menial jobs to raise her three boys. But on the flip side of the coin, his step brother married a wealthy young woman with money and had one daughter. When his daughter was of age, she was proposed to young barrister and a grand wedding ceremony took place in the village.

Within a few years the young barrister started to drink and little by little gambled all his money and his wife's wealth too. Finally everyone including my grandfather's step brother was on the streets begging for survival. That beggar that day was his step brother. "Kumar, remember you cannot ever build on some ones tears or sufferings." Today those words rang in Kumar's heart, he silently wept for that widow and her children. They rode in silence for a few miles into the jungle. Then suddenly the priest told them to stop. He got off the taxi and bade them good bye. "I am looking for the tree of good and evil, to chop it down, so we humans can not mess with God's laws, he exclaimed, "you know the garden was here". Then with out a word he vanished into the woods. Yes Kumar had heard that legend over and over again in his childhood, but who really thought there will be people looking for the centre of the Garden. Sailors had called this island the pearl of the orient for the beautiful flowers and foliage that enticed them, even the stones were colorful. Kumar and the driver drove in deep thoughtful silence for the next few hours. How did this strange old priest know about Kumar's brush with death or his quest looking for his brother? Everyone seemed to know more of what was going on than Kumar. He felt a little uneasy like everything was preplanned and designed for his arrival, yet he the key player was kept in the dark. Why the long buried memories of his youth and childhood kept surfacing over and over. It seemed like for every step closer to his destination, he was pulled backed into the past two steps back.

Suddenly the taxi came to a stop at a junction where the roads intersected like a cross. "We will stop here for a cup of tea, Sir and I want to worship at the temple for a safe journey." said the driver. Both got out, Kumar walked towards the little tea shop and ordered two cups of tea and some lentil donuts, picked his order, paid and pointed to the driver who was just breaking a coconut and saying his prayers to god in the tiny temple. The shop keeper nodded, and Kumar walked away from the tiny group of people to find a quiet place to enjoy his tea and short eats. As he started to enjoy, he noticed the jungle close to the road and the huge trees were full of brown monkeys waiting for the passersby to throw their scraps of food to feed them. Theses monkeys seem to be curious of this man coming to close into their comfort zone, so they seem to be chatting and swinging from branches, then swinging back to lower branches. "Alms" heard Kumar.

Chapter 9 ......

Sage by the rest stop

There stood a tall, yet thin man with matted hair, draped in long off yellow robes, hands reaching out. Kumar immediately pulled a few rupees and tried to hand it the sage. "No my boy, I will be happy to have what you do not finish" he said pointing to the half empty cup of tea that sat on the ground next to Kumar's feet and the half eaten lentil cakes still hiding in the banana leaf, packet. "Sir," Kumar addressed the sage, "I have already soiled theses with my touch, and it is not good for you, I will buy you some fresh food". The dark eyes of the sage twinkled with laughter, "So my boy, you think you can infect me, the only infection that you give me is your kindness". He reached picked up the cup of tea and slipped it gingerly, relishing every drop of lukewarm liquid. Silently, smiling Kumar handed him the left over lentil cakes. After a few minutes eating he looked straight at Kumar and asked "So my boy, you have come home to find your heart's desire?" Kumar seemed to be taken back at the directness of this sage and immediately denied with a vehement "No sir, I am as confused as to why or what made me return to this part of the world." The sage smiled, and said gently "You are right boy, there is a lot of confusion, if you do not listen to your soul, the universe has a way of weaving your path to lead you to your soul's desire, as we call it our destiny, your soul has been wondering for many lives looking for it's real heart's desire, and till you rectify the pain you caused to some other soul, you will search for the answer and peace, but you are almost at the end of your journey. Remember to reach your destination you may have to glance at the past. Not only to remember where you came from but also learn from those experiences. Every thing a soul goes through in each life time makes you stronger and braver." Kumar was more confused now. Kumar remembered the old priest's words a teacher will come when you are ready. Kumar was determined to find out more. "Sir, please explain what you mean, I was lead to believe that when we die our life ends". The sage looked as he was in a trance. He cleared his throat and smiled. "Boy, the universe is an immensely loving and giving spirit. When we transition, our souls reach a plane where they take account of their past life and see what more they can learn or if their had found their desire. The soul is an ever growing entity. So to fulfill it's new desire or need it choose how and where to be born, and who its earthly parents are going to be. Theses earthly people are the most helpful for the soul to learn its lesson. Some souls are looking for wisdom and some are looking for their soul mates to complete them. As you are almost to the end of your journey you will taken back in your mind's eye to your past lives to remind your strength and the lessons you have learned. This is to give you the courage you need to achieve the ultimate goal. You feel tired and confused, you heart feels heavy, you want to end all this and die. You are not afraid of death. Theses are sure signs of reaching the end of your journey. The next few hours you will drift into scenes of your past lives, some of which will make sense, some will not make any sense. But you were there. You may not recognize yourself in theses episodes. All you have to do is to keep an open heart and put away all the trash you have collected in your educated brain. Sit still and flow with your soul's flight into the past. You will fly back into time till you are ready to meet the present. Then the universe will send another messenger to lead you over the threshold." the stranger replied. Kumar was drawn into this man's web of words and said that he had not come to find any answers for his tired life, but to rescue his brother. The sage looked at Kumar and went on to expound. "Boy, sometimes the reason for our journey in life has no bearings to where and why we undertake such journeys.

Kumar was silent. Kumar wondered if this religious man even knew about his homosexual life style, and the Christian faith has branded him unclean and tarnished. The sage seemed to read Kumar's mind and said. "Yes boy, and there is no harm or no shame in loving an other man. Love in any form is sacred. The universe is full of love you just have to open your eyes, as a boy when you milked a cow or a goat you made love to the animal. That is why your pail was always full of milk. When you planted a garden it bloomed to its fullest, to return its love to you. Even the boots you wear is making love to you, keeping your feet warm and clean, just like mother earth keeps mine. Love is a sacred gift, unfortunately very few beings know how to see and enjoy it. When love is full in your being you can only bring love out. That is why your lover has pined for you, and searched for you so many lives. This time you will connect, so do not worry about what I or any one tell you, just be silent and let your soul lead you. I rejoice for you my son. Now unless you have any questions I must be on my way". Kumar was fascinated by the sage's prediction, and said "Yes sir I have a question, why did not you take the money I offered you". "My mother universe provides for me, I do not need to waste my time with material things, but make love to her and her creation." He replied and bowed clasped both his hands to say "Namaste and parted." Kumar returned the greeting.

Chapter 10 ......

A steps closer to the first glance into the past

Kumar walked and got into the taxi, without even saying another word to the driver, who was already in and ready to roll. There was something a little strange in the driver's demeanor. He seem to be aging and hunching, May be the journey is making him tired Kumar brushed that thought and tried to get comfortable on the back seat. His heart seemed to be restless and so he could not find a comfortable position to sit, nor did he want to engage the driver in meaningless conversation. Kumar kept playing his conversation with the sage in his mind over and over. How did he suspect Kumar's sexual desires? How did he relate every thing in life to a sexual dance? All theses thoughts kept Kumar's head spinning. They were now driving through thick jungles; huge trees formed a canopy over the black winding snake like road. Sun light just leaked ray by ray between the heavy foliage. Yet Kumar felt there were eyes watching him. The hair on the back of his neck stood and he felt a sudden chill run down his spin. This is what I need now Kumar thought to himself and pulled the old blanket next to him to cover himself. The driver noticing this wound the widows up and shut them almost tight. Such a sweet man, Kumar thought, I would love to seduce him, but not here nor not this time. Kumar's mind ran back to his home and to his art of seduction. He would invite his prey to his home, have soft music playing, candles dimly lighting his living room. After they look each other over and see the sexual attraction they would smoke a joint, and slowly Kumar would disrobe and dominate the man's manhood, by entering him and becoming one, locked in tight embraces and deep tongue sucking kisses. Kumar left his penis stir in his jeans, and rubbed it down with his hand, thinking, when will I go back home and enjoy this type of pure pleasure? Kumar was brought back to the reality of the moment when he heard the driver say "Sir, we will stop at this place, for an hour or so as I am getting very tired. You will love to see Sigiria the fort and painting of our ancestors." He drove the taxi to dirt parking lot and pointed to the paths that lead to the old mountain fort. There were many people or tourist walking down that path, so Kumar followed them, still lost his own world of thoughts. Sigiria is a tourist attraction for the beautiful original paintings done on its fresco many thousands of years ago. Kumar had seen it and studied the story behind this mountain fort. At the entrance of this attraction, there were many guides and groups getting ready to climb the steep stairs to the fresco and the fort ruins on the top. The tourist department had built a much comfortable staircase with hand railing than what was there some 50 years ago when Kumar went to see it as a boy. Kumar stood wondering if he should join any of the groups to go up, when he felt a tug on his sleeve. There stood an old woman neatly dressed in a white sari and blouse, with a part of her sari draped over her head motioning Kumar to follow her. What do I have to loose Kumar thought and followed her. "I will tell you, the history of this place just for one rupee, my boy" she said and smiled broadly. "Only one rupee, I will give you five". Kumar replied. She motioned him to follow her away from the crowd, found a secluded spot and sat down on the ground and motioned Kumar to sit down. Uncomfortably Kumar squatted on the ground next to this regal woman who, sat flat on the ground with her legs crossed and straight in a very lady like position.

"This my boy is one of the puzzles to your nightmare" she started, "The king who ruled this country had his capital city few miles north of this stone hill. He and his two sons came around here to hunt and frolic many times. Then one day the king got some news about some one trying to invade this country, so he dispatched his eldest son with the army to fight the invaders. While the army and the crown prince was away the second boy Kymunu, killed the father and crowned himself king. But being afraid of his brother's return came to this rock and built his castle on top, with a small piece of land to grow rice and fruits a stable and barn for horses and cows, a pool for water and quarters for his servants and guards. Since there was no water up on the rock the servants carried it on their heads and climbed the steep chipped steps to fill the king's pool. Firewood and all other creature comforts was carried piece by piece to make the little but lavish palace comfortable and beautiful. On the other side of this rock hill is a small cave, where the king kept a watch man to be the look out. The king moved his queen and her maids to the castle and ruled from here. His citizens were terrified and called the "evil Kymunu, or Thuta Kymunu". The new young King felt safe in his palace and was content. The guard, who sat day and night as a watch man, got bored so started to play his flute. He was supposed to have even awoken the Gods with his talent and the whole world became silent to listen to his beautiful music. Many of the locals believed this man was a reincarnation of the Lord Krishna, a Hindu god who also played his flute to seduce the pretty maidens of the village. The queen and her maids heard this heavenly music and came down secretly to spy on the musician. Unknown to the queen the guard saw her and was attracted to her beauty fell madly in love with her. But he realizing his lowly status kept his heart's desire to himself. The queen's maid too fell in love with guard and did seduce him and smuggled him into the queen's chambers many a night. The guard although had no contact with the queen started to paint her partially nude form on his fresco wall. He would search for roots and plants make color dyes and spent hours recollecting his vision and painted the queen's portrait on the walls. The guard spent his time pinning for the queen's love and playing his flute melancholy music. He painted many different poses of the queen from his heart. The maid who was enjoying a sexual tryst with this guard wanted his heart and body, the king was fearful of his brother, kept focusing on saving his kingdom. So four humans formed a rectangle pulled at each corners. The guards lowly birth status was a big barrier to even approach or let the queen even suspect his burning desires for her. So he painted every part of her beautifully body on the fresco wall. Then all hell broke loose, the rumors that the brother had massed a large army and was marching to fight his brother to regain his lawful throne, sent waves of fear and commotion in the royal household. The maid accidentally saw the wall murals of her lover's handiwork. Burning with anger and bitterness she betrayed her innocent mistress, to her master the king. Kymunu, angry and unable to believe his wife's faithfulness disguised himself as a commoner and went to the watch out point to see, if this stories were true. He was stunned at the paintings. So he marched up to his palace and accused his queen, who was completely lost and puzzled. He dragged her down to the fresco, and showed the paintings. The queen was stunned but secretly her heart jumped with joy to see the careful adoration and love poured into this work of devotion. She pleaded with the king to forgive the creator of this art. The king with his disloyal heart only saw disloyalty so he ordered the guard to be thrown from that high cliff. As his last request the guard kissed the queens feet, turned jumped to his death, the kiss sent a chill into the queen heart. She too ran behind the guard and jumped to her death. Needless to finish the story the king was captured and killed. The brother took his rightful throne. The maid lost her mind and became a destitute. So now you want to know why I am telling this sad story with out the trimming we give our tourist. You are here to see which role you played in that crumbling saga I have waited all theses years to rectify my hurtful error, and today I can return in peace." Kumar for a moment was taken aback, this woman is mentally deranged, and I should give the money and walk away. But before Kumar could even move, she touched his hand, and said "how many stars have to shine and die, before you go home, go to the top of the rock, on the right corner there is a small dirty pond, sit next to it very quietly and look in the water and some of your questions will be answered, then you can come and pay me. I have done my part, now I can go in peace". She bowed clasped her hands and walked away from him without turning her back to Kumar. Her face was streaked with tears. Even then Kumar did not realize why he felt so drawn to this old creature. I have known her somewhere he muttered to himself and went to test her theory.

On the top, he shied away from others and found the little dirty pool and looked into the muddy algae grown shallow water, and stood still. Suddenly the water cleared and the story he heard was been acted to him by the original cast, women and men in royal garbs, walked around to pay respect to their king and queen. The royal couple was surrounded by their servants and slaves, and then Kumar saw the maid sneaking in the guard. The guard looked straight into Kumar's eyes. A cold chill ran down Kumar's spin. Is that me? how and why his head raised and the water ran muddy again. The maid, who leading the guard was the old woman at the foot of the mountain. Suddenly Kumar realized why she waited for him. Kumar rushed back to the spot where he had left the old woman. She had questions to answer but she was no where to be found. Was this one of past life experience, is this why I am so fond of music and art. Do the traits of your past life follow you in very birth? Questions kept running in Kumar's head. Was the old woman the maid come to rectify her errors? More questions. No one to enlighten his search for answers. Kumar felt dejected and tired. The thought that the answers lied within you kept ringing in his ear.

Kumar walked and got into his taxi, and collapsed on the back seat. Kumar heart was heavy, tears just steamed down his cheeks. "Sir if you eat some fruit and close your eyes you will find peace" the driver muttered and the taxi purred.

Chapter 11 ......

Into the deep silence...an other glance into the past

Kumar leaned back squinting his eye lids to hold the stream of tears welling in his eyes, as he felt in the basket to pull out a ripe mango. He massaged the fruit, and bit the end and through that end sucked the soft sweet pulp of the mango. As the sweet nectar of the fruit flowed down his throat and the tears down his cheeks, he suddenly felt like he was descending into a dark precipice. Then he saw a small yet beautifully formed white lotus flower floating on a narrow clear stream. The stream seems to run through a well fortified castle. The entrance of the castle was heavily guarded and the soldiers seem to be thorough in searching anyone who entered the castle. There in lived a handsome prince, almost kept captive by his parents the king and the queen. Just before the birth of the prince, the queen had a strange dream. She was warned that this prince will not follow in his father's foot steps but become a grater king and lead a very simple poverty stricken life. So the royal parents kept the crown prince in the castle and exposed him only to the beautiful things of life. The prince never saw old people, poor hungry people or witnessed death. One day while walking in the place gardens, the prince spied a small door leading into the woods. That night when every one was a sleep the prince escaped to explore the world outside his castle. There he ran in to a band of gypsies resting by their camp fire singing and dancing. There the prince saw this beautiful gypsy girl Anarakali and fell madly in love with her. The couple kept their tryst a secret and the prince would contact his lover by sending messages floating on white lotus. Kumar had heard in his childhood that the goddess of enlightenment floated on white lotus flowers. As he followed the floating flower, Kumar heard sweet yet a melancholy music. There at the lower end of the stream sat a beautiful young gypsy decked in all her finery and a small lean boy playing a harp. As Kumar reached to pluck the lotus out of the water, the lean yet beautifully henna decorated hand of the woman snatched it. In the lotus was hidden a small yet highly decorated capsule. She gently opened and pulled out the flimsy parchment and read the message. Joy filled her face she started to dance and sing around the boy harp player. Kumar then noticed that the boy was blind yet he laughed and kept on playing his harp. The young women dragged the boy and whispered in his ears and ran down to the small gypsy camp. Kumar followed the boy and then the troop of the gypsies towards the entrance of the city. The troop was full of joy and danced and sang as they approached the castle gates. The guards opened and accompanied the troop of gypsies to the palace court yard. The group stared to entertain the royal family. The young woman started her song and dance routine, and Kumar noticed that her eyes were focused on the young prince sitting next to the majestic king. As Kumar was enthralled by her song "Love is never easy…." The night before the prince had pleaded with his parents to give permission for theses gypsies to entertain them. The king reluctantly agreed but knew something was a miss. When the king realized how mesmerized his son was with this young gypsy, he screamed with a sheer anger and called his guards to arrest the young gypsy. The king accused her of hypnotizing and seducing his son, and sentenced her to be banished. The prince pleaded with his father to spare the love of his heart. The king decided to entomb the woman in the place garden so the prince will know not mix with the wrong crowd. The masons came and as the gypsies watched in horror, as the guards tied the young woman to a pole and stared to build a tomb around her. She kept on singing "Love is never easy…." As the brick wall rose all round her and her blind brother kept on sobbing and playing his harp. The prince stood stunned and unable to move, paralyzed with sadness. Kumar looked at his face with drying tears and kept trying to recollect where he had seen that face. By now the guards were chasing the gypsies out of the city. Kumar followed the blind harp player as he was dragged out of the city. The boy sobbing loudly called out "Gautama, I will not live in this land and started to stumble down the street. "Where will you go, blind fool?" some one cried. "Any where but in this land when kings seduce young innocent maidens and then murder them" he screamed back and started to stumble down the road. Kumar reached out to help him, and felt a gentle touch on his shoulder, "I will watch after your ancestor" said this young woman who was just murdered. Suddenly Kumar realized he was watching his ancestral past unfold. The blind harp player did find his way to the coast of Lanka, played for the king of Lanka and won a portion of the land. There after many centuries Kumar was born. Kumar turned to young spirit and looked at her sad face and inquired, why so much pain? She gently replied "some one has to pay" and vanished. Kumar was stunned again. He did remembered that in silence God speaks so decided to be quiet. Kumar then turned his view to the city wall and saw the young prince in plain clothes with no robes quietly sneaking out of the castle walking out of the city. Then Kumar realized who he was. How our lives are intertwined Kumar thought. Somehow the past and present seem to be connected.

Chapter 12 ......

A different world a different past

Then Kumar was suddenly found himself in a deep forest witnessing a small pale boy collecting firewood, and walking into a small hut. In there was an old man draped in a long rob cooking some rabbit stew on an open fire There was a drastic contrast in the age and looks of both in the little hut. The sage must be very old skin shriveled, eyes half drooping with the years of toil. He seemed to be at the end of long journey, His hair fully gray and thinning. His skin proudly exhibited its age spots. The boys was young, his complexion like peaches and cream, his body was muscular and firm. His ass firm and round protruding as it was inviting attention. The boy's eyes were blue as the deep blue ocean, yet there was so much admiration and love in his eyes for the old sage. Not a word was said but both ate the stew and retired into their pads by the fire to retire for the cold winter night. As the embers of the fire started to die the boy slowly crept into the old man's pad, and snuggled very close to the man, the boy pushed his firm buttocks into the old man's groin. The old man slowly threw his arms and held the boy's chest close to his. The boy felt the growth of the old man's manhood. It grew like a snake and crept its way into the boy's body and spit its love venom. The boys seem to absorb every drop of it. "Arthur, you will never be free of me, of this fate unless you do something heroic" whispered the old man. What am I doing here, invading the tenderest moment between the sage and the boy? Why am I witnessing this scene? Kumar Wondered. Did I play any part in this episode? Is my malady stay with me through all my existence? What type of heroic deed I am called to perform? Once tasting a man's nectar do you stay hungry rest of your life? More questions and no answers.

Chapter 13 ......

The goodbye, another glimpse into the past

Kumar seem to float into the tunnel of darkness again, nothing seem to make sense just more questions and more pain that made his chest swell with sorrow like an over inflated balloon. Then he found himself spying on a strange yet sad scene. Kumar was sitting on the half wall of an open ornate balcony. The little breeze made the sheer white drapes dance in a seductive dance inviting pain and sorrow. As Kumar peeped into the large room, he saw a man in his thirties lay in huge carved bed, next his feet was a young boy in his teens massaging the man's feet very gently. The man looked gravely ill, the boy's almond shaped eyes, was filled with sheer sadness. The man stirred and the boy rose to feed him some liquid from the copper cup next to bed. The boy helped his master gently sip his drink. The man pointed to the balcony and the boy helped him walk to the open air and face the clouded moon. As the two stood, together, the man leaning on the boy and the pillar of the balcony, he started to talk. Kumar moved closer so he could hear what was being said. The man in a raspy voice said "Boy, you have been my slave for the last 10 or so years. You were a gift to me by your father's enemy when I conquered your village and people. Last night I dreamt the goddess of death dancing at my door. My days here are numbered. So I want to take your slave metal collar and set you free". The man seemed to be laboring with his speech. The boy stood motion less. He seemed to be frozen, his pale yellow face turned white as the drapes that were now motionless. Then without looking at his master, he raised his lord's hand and whispered, into the once strong hand that cut down many men in battle, very gently, "My lord, I came to serve, when I do not know and why I could not understand. All I remember was being pried from my mother's arm and dragged into a dungeon, where they took my manhood away. My gentle looks and my smooth skin were a curse to me. I was mauled, ravished, beaten and raped many times by many men that I do not care to recall. I cursed the Gods of my family every waking moment till your army walked and destroy those barbarians. To pacify your anger and destruction they offered me to you. Those barbarians believed I could calm your anger. I wanted you to thrust your bloody sword and put an end to me, and my wretched existence. But you took me into your care. I traveled with you cleaned, robed and fed by you. I slept at your feet night after night but you never even looked at me. I bathed you and purposely fondled your man hood, oiled your beautifully muscular body, shaved your face and robed you. I even jealously watched you let your friend enter and enjoy your manhood. I cleaned the stains of his and your sweet secretions. I even secretly tasted yours. It was several moons later you took me into your bed and entered my body, with so much gentleness, I came alive. I watched and followed you into battles half way across this great land; I stood silently and held your hand when your desires wanted other men or women. I also know the fear and hate others in your court felt towards me. A stranger like me around a great lord like you, sharing your intimate moments, lying in your arms and they all saw the affection you have towards me. You my lord have been my shield and protector." The boy chocked, tears ran down his face like a torrent river. "What freedom do I need with out my lord; I have given myself completely body and soul to you. Please my lord, thrust your sword into my chest and free me, so that I will be with you as you enter the house of your gods." The man's face was torn with anguish, he sobbed uncontrollably. Then in a quiet but clam tone the man turned to boy, put his arms around him, lifted his face to him and gently laid his dried and fever torn lips on the boy's narrow pink lips. With laboring breath, he said "I am full of gratitude and love for my gods for sending you into my life boy, I will plead with them, that you be with me forever". The boy knew he had to lead his master back to his couch. The doors of the chamber flew open; there stood the master's lady with a host of physicians, priests and soldiers. The boy slowly very stealthy moved into the shadows of the room. The crowd hovered over the sick man whispering and nodding as the tried to diagnose and help this dying worrier. He had brought them all their wealth and power, now him gone they will be destitute. They need someone to blame for their dooming misfortune. The woman already had a plan hatched in her mind. She scanned the room and pointed to the boy, who was hiding in the shadows. The soldiers grabbed him, and lead him out. He looked at his master, who laid half a sleep burning with fever and walked very silently out. They marched the boy into inner sanctum of their temple, where human or animal sacrifices are performed. They stripped him nude, the temple maidens anointed his smooth and young body with perfumed oil. They sneered at his groin, as he did not have any testicles, which was removed when he was castrated so many years ago. "Gods would love this freak" they laughed to themselves and laid him on a stone table. The boy waited for the priests to start the ceremony and send him to his master's side. He closed his eyes and for the first time in his life whispered a prayer of gratitude to his master's gods. The room was dark and suddenly became deathly quiet. The boy heard the huge doors creaking shut and then he smelt the all too familiar breathe. He opened his eyes in terror; there stood his master's male friend half robbed with a fiendish grin. "I have watched you give your self to your lord without reservation, now it is my turn boy." He then forced the legs of the boy open, pushed his middle finger in the boy's pink but tightly shut ass hole. The boy was paralyzed with fear, history is repeating it's self in his life time twice, he thought why? The older man lifted the boy like a straw doll and slides him onto his erect manhood with sheer force. The boy's body withered in sheer pain. The boy then bit the man's thick lower lip and made blood gush out of it like a fountain. This seem to excite the abuser even more, he thrust his groin harder and harder into the boy, till all the flood gates opened and he filled the boy with all his male juices. "Now you can go to your lord" said the old solider and broke the boy's neck like a dry twig. He held on to the lifeless body still resting on his oozing man hood for a few more seconds till it turned stiff, then laid it on the stone table, spit the blood in his mouth on the dead boy's face and walked out. Kumar stood the shivering at man's cruelty and unable to fathom the scene and his connection to it. Did I play a part in this saga? Kumar wondered. If so what role did I choose to be born as? Kumar felt the weight of the world seem to crushing his heart and squeezing very drop of pain out of his soul.

Chapter 14 ……

Bound for eternity… A different life
a different time, another past life experience

Kumar suddenly found himself riding in the third cart pulled by four huge buffalos in a caravan of ten or so carts winding down a narrow hill region in some remote part of the world. It took some time for Kumar to realize that this was the hill country of Sri Lanka, and some wealthy man is making a pilgrimage. Kumar was in the cart of the musician's family. The parents both were in the front of the cart driving the buffalos, two young beautiful girls, the daughters dress in finery, were the dancers and a young dark skinned boy the singer with a sweet melodic voice humming and peeping through the heavy curtain of the back of the cart. The boy caught Kumar's eyes, as the boy hummed and rehearsed his tune, he moved with the grace of the panther inside the cart. He kept tugging and teasing his sisters, as he mimicked their facial expressions. "Vishnu, stop bothering your sister", the woman in the front will call back to the boy. He then will creep back to the cart and slowly peep at the drivers of the cart behind them. The two men driving the cart will expose their groin, and make motion for the boy to join them. Vishnu will blush and withdraw into the cart. As the caravan reached the shores of the island, the leader and rich man, ordered them to set camp for the night, while his servants set out to hire boats to carry them across the Indian Ocean during the day light. Small tents were set up carts were parked, animals were fed and camp fire was burning brightly, food was served and the evening entertainment started when, the servants returned with some bad news. A strong hurricane had hit the little village and destroyed the entire village, the huts and boats. The villagers were helpless, sick and now unable to provide transportation for this man's pilgrimage. The leader now came into Kumar's view, he was in his late forties a very regal looking man, dress in the finest silks but most of all had a kind and compassionate face. He was carrying a silk purse in his waist, he pulled that out and opened and poured the contents on his hand. There were 3 big Rubies mined in the hills of the island. "Let us help theses poor people build their lives back, take one of this semi precious stone, sell and buy food and materials to help build the village." He ordered and returned into his tent to study his charts.

Early morning the people of this caravan joined the villagers to help build the village. Every one was assigned to a task. Vishnu was sent to help a group weave coconut palm leaves into mats to thatch the roof tops. As hard as he tried he was unable to control the leave blades and the spine of the leaves cut his delicate fingers. The others in the group made fun of his predicament. Then Vishnu noticed a boy a few years older than him sitting in the far end, doing the same task with much ease and speed. There was something awkward or different about this boy. No one engaged him in conversation and seems to stay away from his path. The boy motioned Vishnu to move close to him, and Vishnu, against the protest of the others dragged his leaf and sat beside him. The boy, with out raising his head or looking at Vishnu said under his breathe, "Imagine in your head, that you are making the perfect mat, and your hands will follow, then softly sing your favorite love song for me ". Vishnu loved the boy's raspy voice, dug deep within his heart and sang a sweet melody of lost love, as he moved his fingers to dance on the palm leaf to weave his mat. Vishnu did not and could not see his fingers as tears clouded his eyes, as he sang to this stranger. Time flew and the sun was setting. The day's labor was coming to an end. As Vishnu rose to leave the boy grasped his ankle and said, "Now it is pay back time, come with me to my hut, and sing for me tonight." A chill ran down Vishnu's spine, mustering all his strength and he replied "I have to ask my parents permission." "Go, I will wait here for you" ordered the boy, still sitting crunched not looking up. Vishnu ran to his mother and started to beg her for permission. Kumar stood by the boy as he kept on working, He was bony yet tall. The sun had baked him well so his skin was black as the midnight, yet there was certain cockiness about him. I have seen him some where Kumar thought to himself. Vishnu approached the boy and whispered, "My parents want me to ask permission from our master, the Magi" "Come lets go" said the boy and stood, held Vishnu's hand and almost dragged him to the camp. The Magi's servants inquired why the boys were there and informed them, the master was in deep meditation and can not be disturbed. The boy looked up for the first time and the servants froze, "He has the evil eye!" they exclaimed and ran to call their master. Kumar and Vishnu too only now noticed that one of the boy's eyes was grey. The Magi walked out in front of the servants to inquire what the boys wanted. Vishnu mumbled his request. The magi turned to the boy and raised an inquiring look, and before he could ask his question the boy answered, "Sir we belong together, so we have come for your blessing, we will work for you when the sun is lighting the shy, but when He goes to sleep, his sons need to retire to our bed for our rest." The Magi waved his hands bidding the boys to follow their wish and turned into his tent. The boys ran down to the jungle to the boy's broken down hut. The boy took a sea shell and poured some warm rice into it and gave it to Vishnu, who sat mesmerized. The boy sat opposite Vishnu, held his face in his hands and a whispered "I was born like this, I never saw my mother nor do I know my father. The villages claim my mother was impregnated by an ape, and an old witch raised me, in this hut, she died many moons ago, I can see into the past as well as the future. I did try to warn the village of the disaster but fear of me and their greed kept them from taking any precautions. I have seen you, and we do belong to each other. We were together but our pride and jealously separated us. We have been together in many lives, and in many different forms and were separated but we come to connect again and again. I do not know why the gods want to bring so much pain into our lives, but our love for each is so strong that neither death nor life can keep us apart completely, Tonight I will enter your body and we will become one, we will bask in each ones love for a few years then fate will separate us." Vishnu sat quietly like he completely understood the boy and reached over and gently fed him a mouth full of the rice and then kissed his mouth, eating the rice from his new friend's mouth, they rolled on the floor and the naked bodies matted themselves and the boy entered Vishnu's body, they became one. They moved like two wild panthers. Kumar suddenly realized the two black cats that claimed ownership in his drive way and demanded him to feed them each morning. Kumar would smile each morning watching those cats play and tease each other in his back yard. Theses boys reminded Kumar of the pure form of love between two beings and enjoyment as they gasped to breathe deeply and feel the love juices flow into each other. How can anyone see ugliness in such passion? Kumar wondered.

Days rolled into months, months tumbled into years, and Kumar suddenly realized how beautifully each boy had turned into young men. Vishnu was slender, dark and had an ass that seemed to own the world. There was gentleness in his brown almond shaped eyes; his lips were lushes and full. The boy with the evil eye was very tall yet muscular and strong. His hair was prematurely gray. His bad or off color eye more clouded gray and misty. They both seem to be very much in love and very virile. At nights, the man will lead Vishnu into the thick jungles to find all sorts of exotic fruits and flower pod or to the lonely beaches to steal a few eggs from the huge sea turtles that came ashore to lay their eggs. During the day they kept to themselves but worked furiously to complete the village. There was a mutual respect for theses two young men from the whole village. As village grew and was nearing completion the boys turned into men. Now the village was complete. The festival lights were lit to give thanks to the Gods of Land, Sea and Sky. Vishnu's boy soprano voice had turned into a solid tenor voice and his music seems to sound like gods' singing. Every one was enchanted by his voice, music and message. He and his family were in charge of the entertainment and worship for the opening festivals. His two sisters have met eligible men and had the blessing of their master, the wise man, to settle down in this village.

The Magi was getting ready to pursue his goal and travel on the very next day. Even the hut the two boys lived seemed to glow with an exceptional aura.

It was early morning of the festival day, Kumar watch the two men as they woke from their night of slumber. Vishnu reached and held the man's erect man hood in his hands then very gracefully slide it into him, and leaned over and pried open the man's dry mouth and pushed his lushes wet tongue to feed him his saliva. They sat in a double lotus position becoming one and oozing with their manhood and feed every cell in their body with each one's love juice. "Tomorrow, we will start a new life." Vishnu whispered. Kumar noticed tears run down the man's eyes, the bad eye seem to turn black. Vishnu licked the man's cheeks and said very gently, "I will be always near you my loved one, so do not fear, we will see wonderful things and visit beautiful places. Most of all I will sing to the great king and we will live in his palace and enjoy all sorts of riches". The man gently nodded closed his eyes tight and kissed and erupted in Vishnu's body with aloud yet agonizing groan.

The village was lit up, incense permeated the air, prayers were being offered, food was being served and Vishnu and his family took the stage to perform. Vishnu sang the melancholy saga of the Goddess Sita, and her love for her lover Rama. Kumar noticed as the festivities got into full swing the man who always stood at a distance slowly withdraw and walked back to his hut. The man seems to be very dejected and forlorn. He laid on back gazing into the shy. Suddenly the wise old man appeared and said, "Forgive my young strange man, Why are you here alone, you should be watching your beloved Vishnu performing?" The man with out turning his head replied, "Forgive me sir, but I could ask you that same question, you are the guest of honor, and it is not charitable for you to walk away". They both seem to touch a mutual cord. The wise man sat down and said, "Something is troubling you my man, may be if you tell me it we may find a way out". A cold breeze blew across from the ocean, in distant they could here Vishnu singing Sita's prayer begging her goddess to make Rama fall in love with her. The man with evil eye turned and stared at the wise man, whose face was full of wrinkles due to the unusual labor he had endured in building this village back. "Sir, you are an learned man, what I am going to say may sound very childish to you, I was born with this deformed eye, but I can see what people, or animals or trees are thinking and also see into the future. I saw the hurricane coming and tried to warn the villagers but they called me devil possessed and drove me out of the village. But I do see the future, you and my loved one are looking for the mighty king. You to pay homage and Vishnu to find favor. Both in the own way is remarkable. I too am looking, but I have found the Mighty king here in this mealy village the, thick jungle, the rough sea and the sandy beaches. But most of all in my loved one Vishnu's heart and soul. When we are as one, I see the Great Spirit in us. So why will I take a chance in risking this. I know I have done some bad things in my past and so I have this curse, but I have been looking for my loved one and I have found him. I am afraid I will loose him in this trip. I also know if I do not go along I will lose Vishnu. So I am in this quandary. I will tell you once, because you asked me why I can not be happy, this trip will leave us blind, voiceless, loosing our mind and destitute. We are searching for something that is already with in us." As the wise man sat stunned, the man with the bad eye wiped his face, and sighed. "Sir I have found my heart's desire and will walk through hell fire with him, I know if I am faithful, our eighth life together we will never be parted." The wise man stood slowly, some how he seemed to have lost his majesty and wisdom in front of this deformed man and his proclamation of love, and staggered back to his seat at the festival. The man sobbed into his hands.

Early next dawn, the catamarans were loaded, Vishnu exhausted by the nights festivities, got into his parents boat and fell asleep. The man with the evil eye stood at the water's edge unsure of his move. Kumar watched him and felt a deep pang of sadness. How quickly we seem to take our love for granted, and are careless with each one's heart. The magi noticing the man and realizing his predicament motioned him to join his boat. The man swam and hopped on to the end of the boat, still unsure of his place or his position. The magi gracefully invited the man to come in, but the man declined and sat in a daze looking back at the beach and his hut. Kumar knew how he felt leaving his home and his surrounding to venture into this unknown journey.

The caravan landed in India, and faced many years of travel. The magi and his servants helped any one and every one who came into their path. They faced many who were starving due to famine and poverty, many who were sick. The magi used his wealth, and tried to ease the pain of theses miserable people. As years rolled on the caravan too lost most of its members. Vishnu lost both his parents, the magi lost most of his wealth and servants, but the man with the evil eye did not leave Vishnu's side. He did say very little, but did love Vishnu like there was no tomorrow.

Finally the caravan dwindles to three members. The Magi with one precious stone as a gift for the Mighty King, Vishnu whose voice sounded like thousand angels and the man whose love for Vishnu grew in leaps and bounds. The three in camels crossed the Khyber Pass into the Arabian Peninsula. Each night the man made love to Vishnu with such a passion that the old Magi would hear their lustful breathing and realize that some thing was going to take place soon. Then one mid day they came across a beaten almost dying woman pleading for water in the desert. The three stopped and helped this poor unfortunate creature, shared their meager ration and water, dressed her wounds and carried her with them till they stopped to rest for the night. During day break the woman told them her story. She claimed to be a high class prostitute and one day fell out of grace and was dragged to be stoned by her own lover, who had first seduced her and then sold her to his friends. While she was waiting for the stones to fall, she was saved by this so called prophet. Now they were killing him for proclaiming to be a king. She had followed the prophet as he was been led to his death, and fell into the hands of the man who wronged her. He claimed to be the new king and was raising an army in secret to fight the Roman invaders. He had recognized and tried to seduce her again, but as she turned away from his advancement, he had gotten angry and raped her. Then he had given his men permission to rape and abuse her. She was left to die in the desert. She told them of a king living a few miles away. Vishnu wanted to visit the king and sing for him. He claimed the king will reward him and then they can return home. The Magi felt the man who was gathering an army was the unknown king; the stars had foretold and wanted to see him. The man with the evil eye said nothing but was determined to be with Vishnu. So the four approached the castle gates. The guards after hearing their story, refused to let all four enter the castle. There seem to a kind of fear among all of them. The youthful look of Vishnu and his sweet voice allowed him to enter the palace. Kumar slid behind Vishnu and saw the court and the King. Although agitated the King did enjoy listening to Vishnu's singing and his dark shiny shin and beautiful face. The King invited Vishnu into his chambers. Vishnu expecting to collect his reward walked in to the chambers to find the King totally disrobed, and legs spread exposing his circumcised wrinkled penis. The King motioned Vishnu to kiss his horrid looking angry little stub, and Vishnu in his youthful innocence laughed and shrugged his shoulders in disgust. This angered the King, he has been rebuked twice this day, once by the so called prophet and now by this strange heathen. The king orders his guards to hold Vishnu down spread eagle and pries the end of the spear into Vishnu's raw asshole, the pain seems unbearable and Vishnu screams shattering very object in the castle. The three outside hear this cry of pain. The man knows and sees what is being done to his lover, digs his eyes out. Blood gushes out, the prostitute and the magi drag him into the desert, fearful of being caught by the guards. There they run into the rebel king, who robes the magi of his only precious stone, drags the woman into his tent, and orders his men to kill the man. The magi finally stumbled to the scene of the crucifixion. There he looks at the prophet on the middle cross and realizes that the man with the evil eye was right, we see god in ourselves and in those around us. The magi feels suddenly all his knowledge was useless and feels that he had completely lost his mind and now was a destitute. Kumar stood silently sobbing. What role did I play or why was I shown this terrible sad saga? Kumar wondered again.

Chapter 15 ......

In the wings of the bald eagle...

Kumar felt he was flying on the wings of a huge bird towards nowhere. Every thing below seemed a daze and moving so fast that he squeezed his eyes and tears rushed out. Suddenly, the bird disappeared under him, and he gently floated down on the wings of the air and came to rest on a peak of small red hill. The color of the soil was blood red, the air was still and dry. The cactus plants looked like lost souls, looking to the shy pleading for drink. Kumar felt the stillness, not a bird was stirring, so he focused eyes to spy on the small pool of water in the valley. In the midst stood a sturdy white wild stallion sipping the warm water to his heart content. He seemed to own the land and the pool. He was such a magnificent creation, Kumar thought, and then he saw a small brown boy lying in the pool, like a dry piece of wood, and very slowly moving towards the hind legs of the stallion. Then appeared on the scene a third person, a rough looking, hairy cowboy who looked tired and his horse seemed to struggle under his master's weight. As cowboy, who roamed the wild seemed to read the signs of nature. His glassy blue eyes scanned the surrounding and he dismounted his horse very quietly, freed his horse of its burden, tied and threw some hay for it to eat and rest. The poor animal seems to read his master's mind very quietly squatted and started to chew on its meal. The cowboy got on all fours and started to creep to the edge of the cliff to see why everything was so quite. He saw the stallion and the Indian boy in the pool of water. By now the boy had floated or moved very near the Stallion. In a flash he reached and grabbed the huge low hanging testis of this stud horse. The stallion shivered and then froze with fear or ecstasy, who could tell. The boy very smoothly untied his narrow leather band and held between his teeth, folded into two with one hand then knotted the stallion's huge nuts and completed his knot. Then slowly reached over sniffed the nuts and bit the skin, till he could taste the blood. Then he slowly withdrew and crawled back to the dry land and collapsed on his stomach. The bright sun shone on his beautiful full round ass, as the loin cloth was sucked into the crake of his ass. The ordeal seemed to suck every bit of energy out of this young boy. The strong stallion stood still and watched this boy. The cowboy slowly crept towards the pool of water. All of a sudden the cowboy leaped and pinned the boy with his weight. The stallion neighed. Before the stunned boy could wake and react to this sudden interruption, the cowboy slides his hands into the groin of the boy and held his small and dainty nuts and penis in his huge hands. "What is good for horse is also good for a wild Indian" the cowboy whispered into the boy's ears. Then the cowboy unbuttoned his pants, pulled out his huge uncut hard penis and thrust it into the boy's tight ass. The boy screamed with pain then, started to whimper as the cowboy pound his dick harder into the boy's ass till he shot his first load. Then he lay on the boy as a man who had conquered the world. "I have fucked many whores boy, but your ass is the best he whispered and sniggered in the boy's ear. Although the boy did not understand, he read the man's body and realized that he was safe under his weight and pounding. The boy pushed his ass into the man's groin and squeezed his ass muscles milking the man's dick. This made the soft dick hard and the pounding and groaning started till the man got rid of his second load. The boy ejaculated into the man's palm and squirmed in delight. The sun was setting and the man rolled over, licked his palm of the boy's juice, smiled and gently turned the Indian's face towards him and kissed him. The cowboy wrapped his hairy manly hands around the boy and closed his eyes and both seem very still and content. The stallion moved out the water and lay next to the couple.

This scene made Kumar simile. The sun set and the shy was covered with stars. A gentle cool breeze blew as if to rock this couple into a deep contented sleep. As dawn broke, the boy slowly slipped away and washed himself in the pool, he then moved like a ghost, and came back with an arm full of ripe apples, part of which he laid by the white stallion. He then crept and positioned himself on the cowboy's thighs and slowly and gently opened his flap and started to gently massage the man's soft dick and low hanging balls. The cowboy stirred and the boy took the man's semi hard penis in his mouth. He pushed the fore skin with his lips gently locked his teeth around the ridge of the cowboy's swelling penis and started to suck it, like he was feeding on his mother's breast, all the while he kept tugging on the man's nuts, twisting it and massaging it. The cowboy moaned and realized that he had never had his manhood played with like this, even the whores he used to frequent, never completely satisfied him the way he was being fulfilled. The boy raised his head and looked straight into the half closed blue eyes of the man, without taking his gaze he pulled out his dagger and flipped his head so his braid of black hair would fly over his shoulder. He cut a few inches of his braid. And used it to tie around the twisted balls of the man, without breaking his sucking movement, the force on his nuts the gentle sucking on his throbbing penis and the teeth lock on his head of the dick, made the cowboy convulsed into a huge volcanic eruption and shoot his load into the boy's throat. The boy slowly kept the movement going on while swallowing the man's seed, and raised his head licking his lips smiling at the cowboy, who was still lingering in a state of ecstasy. The cowboy stumbled to pool and washed himself and silently ate the apples. He saddled his horse and started to ride away, as his horse started to move, the Indian boy sprang on the back of the horse and threw his arms around the waist of the man, sliding them till they rested on the man's crotch. The man smiled to himself thinking strange life is, here no words were spoken, yet the souls seemed to connect. He reached over his shoulder and lifted the boy over his side and placed him squarely between his thighs and snug against his groin. The boy pushed his ass right into his man and they rode over the hills to the cowboy's little shack. The white stallion followed the two men like it was mesmerized.

Then all hell broke loose, they ran smack into a group of red coats. The red coats seeing the Indian fired at the boy and injured both man and boy. The stallion neighed loud and leads the horse with the riders on a fast gallop. The soldiers chased and shot wildly, killing all four the boy, the man and the two horses. Kumar stood paralyzed with fear. What did I do in this scene, was this too one of my past life experience? What role did I play Kumar wondered and searched his grieving heart.

Chapter 16 ......

Slaves of love…

Kumar stood in a large crowd, looking at a stage, where an auction was taking place. The crowd looked blood thirsty and was enjoying the fate of the poor black skinned men and women. Theses niggers seemed completely broken and starved to find a little human kindness. Then they dragged this black man on to the block. He stood tall and muscles ripped in very inch of his body. His eyes were full of hate and fire. His dark lips held closely tight, like holding back his anger which will stream out any moment and singe the crowd to ash. The auctioneer tapped the man's body with a paddle to prove the solid build and strength. The crowd jeered and wanted to see the man's manhood, and the auctioneer stripped the man loin cloth. The balls were like to solid tennis balls stuck high to his groin, and his penis, uncut stood semi hard at around 14 inches long like a police baton. The man did not finch and never lost his far away look. Hate radiated from very pore of his body. Then Kumar noticed an older well dressed white man, leading a half trembling boy by hand to inspect the black slave on auction. "Feel his nuts boy, see if it full of seed to make more nigga babies for you" screamed the crowd. The boy shivered, and stood motionless with his head lowered, but focusing on this huge black man's nuts. The father of the boy, facing the crowd proudly announced that his boy is of age to own his slaves and he was going to purchase his first slave today. The crowd encouraged the boy, who gingerly felt the man's ball, and accidently rubbed his fore arm on the man's fore skin, feeling slight moisture. The boy leaned and whispered into his father's ears, who haggled over the price and the man became the slave of Jimmy Dale Jr. that hour. Jimmy Dale motioned the slave to get into the cart and the group drove back to the Dale family plantation.

The slave Kuttu was in charge of the stables. He was smart and picked up his duties even through he did not understand the strange noise the pale skin owners were making. Kuttu took care of all the horses, cleaned the stable and corral. Kuttu was quick to explore the plantation, and found a stream in the mid of the small forest at the end of the plantation. Kuttu would run like a buck very quietly in the night to the stream and swim in it. He would return to the pad that he put together on the roof of the barn.

Jimmy Dale wanted to ride a brand new black stallion that his grandfather had given him for his sixteenth birth day. The stallion seemed to have a mind of its own. Kuttu watched this strange dance between the horse and the boy. One night, the shy was basking in bright southern moon light, Kuttu was running back from his night bath, completely drenched the scanty lion cloth clinging to expose every inch of man hood, to get into his pad, there stood Jimmy Dale dressed in his riding attire. Jimmy Dale motioned Kuttu for the stallion. Kuttu obeyed and lead the horse into the coral, and kept massaging its neck and making strange noises with his mouth. Jimmy Dale noticed that the horse was not saddled but before he could say or motion Kuttu to saddle the horse, Kuttu picked up Jimmy Dale like a rag doll and placed his on the stallion. Kuttu tried to adjust Jimmy Dale's position on the horse, the horse froze. Kuttu clicked his lips sending a command to the horse. Then Kuttu reached and undid and pulled off Jimmy Dale's boots. Kuttu then pressed Jimmy Dale's bare feet on the side of the horse, and made him hold a handful of the mane hair and clicked, the stallion obeyed and walked very cautiously around the coral at least three or four times. Kuttu lifted Jimmy Dale off the horse and took the horse back into the stable.

Next evening around the same time as Kuttu came running back to the barn, he noticed Jimmy Dale sitting on the fence of the coral covered with a blanket.

Kuttu went into the stables and brought the stallion, lifted Jimmy Dale and went to place him on the horse. Jimmy was butt naked, with his little pecker in erection. Kuttu placed Jimmy Dale on the Horse, put one of his hands around Jimmy's neck and straightened, the boys posture, press the boy's thighs and legs into the stallion's buttocks and slowly licked his huge middle finger wetting it with his thick saliva, and gently lifted Jimmy's ass cheeks and ran his finger between them and then pushed them onto the stallion's back as if to seal them, the boy and the horse into one. Kuttu gave the signal to the stallion which took off into gently trot, then kept building speed. Jimmy Dale was stuck to the horse like white on rice. After an hour or so Kuttu summoned the stallion back to him, and lifted Jimmy Dale of the horse, the boy clung to Kuttu's body. The sweat from Jimmy dale ran down Kuttu's stomach and legs. The slave and the master stayed clinging to each other, and the boy slowly raised his blue eyes and looked deep into the man's brown blood shot eyes. Kuttu carried the boy to roof of the barn and spread his legs and inserted his hard penis into the boy's virgin ass. Kuttu pounded the boy's ass like there was no tomorrow, and Jimmy Dale withered in pure ecstasy. Finally Kuttu moaned as he expelled his nigga seed into the hot ass of his master. At this point who could figure the slave or the master? Kuttu lifted the boy while still in him and stepped over the broom, to signify that from that day on they were one body. Jimmy Dale knew this slave custom and was more than willing to be tied to this nigger.

Kuttu could not penetrate the slave women to get them pregnant, as planned, his huge dick, will be soft as mush and no amount of coaxing will do any thing till Jimmy Dale threw his legs around him he would have an erection that last all night pounding his white boy's ass. Jimmy's father got wind of what was going on and blamed Kuttu for using voodoo witch craft on his boy and had him lynched as Jimmy Dale silently sobbed. Love could never find a happy ending Kumar thought. Did I play a part in this past life episode too? How much pain should one soul experience? Kumar questioned his heart and mind. No answers came out, just a sense of dark melancholy.

Chapter 17 ......

End of the road...

The taxi came to a screeching halt. "We are there Sir" said the driver. He jumped out and started to walk in front waving Kumar to follow. The young driver seemed to have aged or is the evening twilight playing tricks on my eyes Kumar wondered. He was inside the Fort built by the Dutch settlers. This used to be my favorite childhood haunts Kumar thought as he followed the driver into the jungle.

Kumar noticed the driver was scurrying into the jungle on a foot path that was blocked with over grown shrubs, the sun was almost setting and darkness was slowly but surely over taking the sun. Finally Kumar reached a huge flat rock that jutted out like a throne room, stood out of the cliff in majesty and splendor, large over grown trees made a natural roof to keep away the last rays of the fading sun, and a soft sea breeze blew across to cool the area. "Stay here", the driver shouted and disappeared. Kumar sat on the rock and sipped the last drops of water, and gazed at the ocean and beach. Fishermen were roving their boats and small lamps were being lit in the huts to settle in for the night. Kumar try to recollect the reason of his trip to this part of the world, "God I came to save my brother from the terrorist but so far I am having vision of sexual encounters that seem strangely familiar. Where are the men I am supposed to meet and how will it all resolve" Kumar kept asking himself as the dusk settled in. Then suddenly out of no where Kumar heard a gentle tingling of tiny bells, as he strained his eyes into the darkness he saw a row of tiny lamps approaching in a procession. As the group approached Kumar realized it was a procession women dressed in Indian outfits wearing tiny bells on their leg anklets and carrying small lamps. Kumar noticed their figure but could not see their faces as their faces were covered by heavy veils. The lamps reflected on the gold and silver that was interworn into their outfits.

The women surrounded Kumar in a circle and sat down. All raised their hands and said "Namaste" simultaneously. Kumar returned the greeting and asked "Are you the terrorists?" The women laughed, "No sir, we have lived in terror all theses years waiting for your return, your brother is safe with his family now, we used that as a reason to get you back here. Forgive us for our act of deceit but we were unable to find another way to bring you back to rectify the past". Fear gripped Kumar's heart, why am I here? What can I do to rectify the past, what past? Questions ran amok in his head. "Sir, we will explain all that", the leader said very gently, "but first we have to get you ready for the occasion. Sir you have to remove your western clothes, very scrap of it and wear this leather loin cloth, tie this leather head band and this tiny gold anklet with the small bell on your left ankle." Kumar knew he better obey so he stood and stripped his jeans shirt socks underwear and shoes and pushed them into his nap sack. The leather lion cloth fit him like a glove, and then two women approached him with a small copper container and drain the honey like liquid and massaged it into every part of his body. The aroma of the oil filled Kumar's nostrils and almost relaxed very muscle in his body. They threw a Jasmine garland on him. Strange Kumar thought am I getting married or getting sacrificed, I have no way out so lets play along, who will hear my cry for help in this god forsaken part of the world and who will care?

Then the leader of the troop motioned Kumar to sit on a soft pillow and said, "We have a few hours and I am going to tell you the story of our past and you will understand why you are the only one who can change the curse.

She in her gently yet in a musical voice proceeds to tell her story. In the beginning Brahman placed the Garden of Eden in this small but secure island surrounded by the ocean. All plants and animals of all shapes were placed here, and humans were put here to care and tend to them. Every thing flourished and lived a very contented life. Brahman was pleased with his creation and went off to visits other worlds. Then slowly trouble started, humans started to abuse the land the plants and especially the animals. Monkeys became their main target; they will catch them and rape them over and over. As monkeys were much closer to humans, a new generation of half monkey half human was born here. That is our beginning sir, we became target of their abuse as our bodies were like humans but our face were like the monkeys. Humans made us slaves, abused us so much that finally we gathered on the top of the tallest hill in this island and cried out to Brahman to save us. We stayed there for forty days and nights pleading and begging for relief. Finally Brahman came down, and listened to out tale of grief. His foot imprint is still found on top of the mountain, which you call as Adam's Peak. The Almighty agreed to free us by giving us power to grow wings like birds and fly away from the garden, we each could take only three things with us, any thing other than that will not let us get airborne. We in return promised THE Almighty that we will serve him any time he called on us, as a group or individually. So as a group we decided to carry three different plants from the garden and fly away into the North by next day. Early next morning we left all two thousand of us. We requested the king of the birds the majestic white eagle to help us find our new home. He lead into the deep jungles of north India, a hidden valley surrounded by tall snow covered mountains. We made our new home and built our city for us, planted the plants we carried from the Garden of Eden. We named it the city of monkeys, where we jointly decided to dig deep within our souls and bring out the beauty that lay hidden in us. We excelled in the arts. Music, dancing, painting and magic flourished. We also realized that sex was a key ingredient in ones happy life. So we explored every aspect of sexual fantasies. We even wrote the first manuscript on how to live a fulfilled sexually active life, with what Brahman had blessed us with. Our city was filled with laughter, joy, music and love. We also never forgot our great creator Brahman and worshipped him in music and prayers every dawn and dusk. Our prayers rose like smoke and filled the heavens. So the gods started to visit our city, to be entertained, and we were always thrilled about their visits and treated them royally. On one such visits the gods witnesses two of us making love and embraced in a deep tongue twisting kiss, and feeding on each other's saliva that mixed to form sweet nectar. The Gods want to experience that taste but were unable to do so. They approached The Almighty Brahman about this issue. He informed that this special nectar is only produced in the mouths of two earthly beings when they give of themselves to each other unselfishly. He called it the food of Gods-"Amirtham". If Gods was to feed that they have to be born as earthly beings. We also realized sex was a great tool to soften cruel humans, so we would go into the world take different forms and soften men's harden heart by making them enjoy the sexual pleasures. You may have heard of many of your clan, such as the Jewish slave girl Esther, or many of the characters you saw on glance in to your past life experience. Our leader was Anuman, a strong male monkey and you my sir were his love child. You excelled in all the arts and in the art of sexual pleasures. You have lived many lives and did witness some of them on your trip here. She came to a stop and offered Kumar a goblet of sweet coconut water. She sat very quietly to let the story sink into Kumar's confused brain. Kumar sat very still like he was stunned.

Then she leaned forward and continued her story. The second part of the story is how we fell out favor with Brahman, she sighed. Brahman's four sons who wanted to visit the earth and see how things were run by the humans who had also scattered around the mother earth, and set up small kingdoms. All four boys were born as princes to a kind king with three wives. Rama the oldest was the first born, then Parathan the second born to the king's second wife, and the youngest two were born as twins to the third wife. Luxuman was the last born of the twins. The four boys grew and became handsome men. In another kingdom the goddess Sita was born as a princess, she was the god wife of Rama in heaven. When it was time for Sita to marry the news went to all neighboring kingdoms and princes from far and wide came to win her hand in marriage. Of course Sita choose Rama and the couple was married and returned to Rama's father's kingdom. Things were normal till the old king became fragile and wanted to hand over the responsibilities to the one on line for the throne, Rama. As the king and his ministers were training Rama for his new roll, there was a storm brewing in the king's household

Chapter 18 ......

Fulfilling a promise...

When the now ailing king was a young athletic hunter, one day he took his second wife or mistress to hunt and enjoy the nature. The couple was very much in love and threw caution to the wind as they sang and rode thru the forests. Suddenly they rode right into the middle of herd of ruthless and ferocious wild hogs, which charged the king's horse. The king was thrown off his horse and the hogs were charging towards him. His young second wife drew his sword and step in front of the herd. She single handedly fought the herd, killed the leader of the pack and rescued the king. That night when she was dressing his wounds and massaging his sore body the king turned to his love and gently asked her to request anything in return for her saving his life. She thought about this and gently replied that she would remember and ask him to fulfill his promise some time in the future. Years had passed now the king is fragile and lying on his death bed. His second wife enters the king's chamber and sits at his feet and reminds him of this promise that he made her long time were go, when they were young and vibrant. The king wanted to all scores right before he follows the God of Death Yaman into the after world and was more than eager to grant her wish. She gently raised her tear filled eyes, looking lovingly into the frail face of the king said, "Sir, you brought me into your household from a far way land, You already had a queen, I although was a princess became a mistress, always took the second place in all the royal functions, but your love kept me fulfilled and happy. Now you are leaving me in this strange land of your fathers, where I will always be a stranger. I am afraid for my life and my son's life. You are making your first born the king, although I love him like a son, he is not my flesh and what will be our fate after your departure. We will be banished from this land, where I have lived and served you for so many years. I came here as a mere young 14 year old bride, now I am old and I have shed my youth and beauty along the way. So I am claiming the promise you made to me in our youth. Make my son Parathan the monarch and banish your eldest son Rama into the jungle for 25 years".

The king was stunned at this request, but he also knew his second wife's determination, and he being a man of his word agreed to fulfill the promise. Next morning the king summoned all his ministers and his three wives and four sons to his bed chambers. There on his death bed, he handed the throne to puzzled Prathan, banished Rama into the jungle, made all his officials to adhere to his death bed request and die with a broken heart. The four sons were stunned at this request, Rama being an obedient son, made plans to leave the kingdom immediately after he had performed his last rites to his father. Sita decided to accompany her husband. Parathan refused to sit on the rightful throne of his elder brother, but agreed to rule the country sitting below the throne, on which he laid Rama's shoes. Luxman decided to accompany the couple into the jungles, as he could not spare to be separated from his older brother. The kingdom not only mourned for the death of the just king, but for loosing the crown prince. After performing their duties the threesome went into the deep jungle to survive. Here they built a small hut and fended for themselves. Life was simple but yet joyful with out all the royal glamour.

One morning Rama ran into a young woman singing dancing and collecting flowers. Rama was mesmerized by the sweetness of her voice. The young woman was a sister of the Sri Lanka King, who was able to fly in her flying chariot and visit exotic places. The young woman fell madly in love with Rama as soon as they eyes met. She tried to seduce Rama, who very rudely shunned her. Heart broken and insulted she returns to her island home with vengeance in her heart. She started to poison her brother's heart, with lust and craving for Sita. She describes Sita as the paragon of virtue and a woman fit to be his queen. So both brother and sister hatched a plot to kidnap Sita while the men were out haunting for their daily meal. While Sita was doing her morning prayers, the king of Sri Lanka forcefully carried and flew with her in his flying chariot to his palace and imprisons her in his palace garden. This is where you are sitting now. While flying over the Indian Ocean, Sita lost her marriage symbol "thalie" a thick, long solid gold chain with seven pendants in shape of beetle leaves. Each pendant symbolized the commitment the couple made to each other.

Kumar now started wonder how this story was going to wrapped round him at the present. The woman paused and pointed to the first star that appeared on the black sky. "We will give thanks our ancestors who are watching over us all theses life times". The women turned and started a sweet sounding chant; Kumar moved his left ankle and the tiny bell started to accompany theses women in singing too. Kumar watched as the stars filled the sky and blinked in anticipation trying to figure out if any one of the stars were really his ancestors.

The woman cleared her throat, and started her story. She very quietly said this part is where you come in my sir, so please pay close attention to it. Kumar stiffened a little, and then felt the calmness of these women around him. Kumar relaxed. Rama returned to their humble abode to find it destroyed and Sita missing. Even the alter to her God Krishna was in a disarray. So Rama and his brother Luxman, started to search for Sita, suspecting foul play they inquired from trees, animals and humans. They put the few clues together and started to follow the path Sita was carried. Since Rama could not return to father's kingdom, he had to recruit a make shift army. Every farmer and ordinary human picked up what ever instrument they had and followed Rama to help him right the wrong. It was an army of an unfit group if ever there was one, except they all had one goal in heart.

They all wanted to make right what was a great injustice. The make shift army reached the southern tip of India and faced the blue Indian ocean. Rama was lost and heart broken. With his brother's coaxing he called on his father Brahman to help them. The mighty God called on your father the leader of moneys, Anuman to help. Your father gathered every able body to go to the aid of Rama. You Kumar were just a sprig of a boy, but wanted to help and begged your father to take you with him. Although young, you were very advanced in magic and were able to disappear into thin air or change your form to any other creature you wanted to be. So all of us flew to Rama's camp and discussed the situation. Your father decided to build a bridge to get the make shift army across the Indian Ocean into Sri Lanka. We unearthed huge rocks and carried them on our shoulders and dropped them into the Indian Ocean. The bridge was complete, Rama and his army crossed into Sri Lanka. You can even today see the remnants of this bridge near Mannar, a small costal town in Sri Lanka. You father being a peace loving leader, requested Rama to give him and his group permission to talk sense to the king of Sri Lanka. Rama agreed. Fifty soldiers accompanied your father Anuman to talk with the king. The king disregarded the peace ambassadors, laughed at their sub human form. The king commanded his soldiers to capture monkeys and tie torches to their tails and set them free. Little did this foolish king realize that theses flying monkeys would fly all around his kingdom and set it all a blaze? With out shooting one arrow Rama was declared winner, and he found Sita, unkept and weeping. She had not groomed her long black hair or washed her tear stained face, had not eaten a morsel of food but was in constant prayer to her God Krishna. Her tear stained eyes kept watch on the Indian ocean for her beloved. She sat on this same rock that we are sitting today, many years nothing could move this rock, as it stands for the love the woman carried for her lover and husband. Rama was overjoyed to find his wife Sita, but noticed that she was not wearing his seal of marriage the thali. How ever much Sita tried to explain how she had lost that when she was carried over the ocean, Rama could not believe her. We the monkeys felt our hearts break for the rivers of tears this helpless woman was shedding and felt a kind of remorse towards this perfect being Rama. Finally Sita ordered us to collect dead wood and start a huge pyre, we obeyed. We started a huge pyre and she walked into the blazing fire and came out without a singe, unburned but heart harden she renounced her husband Rama and begged us to carry her into a jungle ashram in India. We obliged and a certain number of us accompanied this broken woman into the ashram to become a hermit. The ones who accompanied stayed with her in the ashram to protect this weak broken woman. Mean while Luxman decided to find the thali. This where you come in, my good man Kumar. The story teller paused.

You Kumar had fallen madly in love with this perfect being Luxman. You although subhuman, loved the way his long black hair cascaded down his broad shoulders, his muscle ripping body, his protruding manhood and his bright green eyes. You had made every opportunity to be close to Luxman, who did not even play you the slightest attention. You were content to breathe his odor and kiss his shadow. So you pulled all your wits and informed Luxman you will enlist the angels of the sea, the dolphins to search for Sita's thali. You changed shape and went under sea to visit the leader of the dolphins and beg for their assistance. They being very compassionate beings agreed to help you and Luxman to find the thali. Luxman moved his camp to this very spot and you agreed to stay with him, and serve him. You father requested us to stay with you. So the long wait started, as the days ran into months you desire for Luxman grew like wild fire. You would do everything possible to make his life comfortable. At nights you would rub his feet and sing to him love songs as he fell a sleep. Little by little your hands will travel up his muscular legs and thighs, till it gently fondled his manhood. Luxman, half a sleep and half sexually starved would accept your advances till you start to perform oral sex on him. He would burst into your mouth and you ate every bit of it. This was not enough for you, you wanted to bear his seed, so using all your magic on a moonless night you changed your self into a beautiful nymph, crept into Luxman's pad and made passionate love to him. As he was just exploding in you, he pried opened your eyes to look into your soul and saw the ugly subhuman monkey boy you were. You had knotted his penis with your tight ass muscle that it was spiting its seamen into you. Luxman was angry at his predicament, wanting you and yet disgusted by you. He with his bare strong hands strangled you, snuffing your life energy. Hate changed Luxman that night into monster and he ran and hid himself into that cliff. She pointed to the rocky cliff behind Kumar. Brahman and the gods were angry with you and us. The sealed the gateway to our home the city of monkeys. We have been roaming with you all theses many lives, trying to find Sita's thali, and a way to rectify the error made by a young one who was madly in love. We knew only you can cure the past, and set Luxman free from his self imposed prison of hate. He has grown hideous and violent. Finally the time is right; we found the thali, during the tsunami. You have to wear this gold chain inside your leather loin cloth, and have to wrap it around both of you. This will release the spell. She handed the thali to Kumar who slipped it, around his waist into his loin cloth. She continued, as a boy your love for this beautiful perfect creature was full of lust and desire, tonight you will meet the same creature in a hideous form, you have to find the lost man and bring him to the open. Only you can find away, so we have watched over you all theses lives. You have felt our presence around you many times. Even lately two black cats came and watched over you, at your home in California. Tonight you have to learn from all your past life experiences and come out of your shell and conquer fear and evil. We will be there but we can not help but send you our blessings. Now before the cliff opens you have a few moments to reflect on what you heard. She suddenly stopped and started softly to chant a prayer and the others followed. Kumar buried his face into his sweaty palms and quietly sobbed.

Chapter 19 ......

Kumar's Prayer...

As the melancholy music and chant from the women sitting around him rose like smoke from an incense lamp, Kumar felt his heart stir with passion, he stretched out his hands opened his palm to face the heavens, which were now studded with a million of stars. Kumar slowly raised his tear strained eyes to the shy and started his heart felt prayer. "Oh! Great Creator of the universe, what ever my fate is in this life, and what ever fate I faced in my past lives, I accept and honor your wish. Please, Origin of love, do not deal the same fate to me. If in your infinite wisdom you feel that I deserve to walk this earth to learn my lesson for seducing your son. Oh! Great god, my heart is dry, my eyes are ever spring well of tears. Please Great One, have mercy on this imperfect being. I know I was conceived in sin and I am not perfect like you, nor I am a perfect human being. I know now I am part ape and part man, this fate I take. It was your source of love that put a spark of love in my sub human heart to seek love, to love perfection. Right or wrong I fell in love with your perfect creation, your son Luxman. Forgive me lord for wanting to love perfection. If one lesson that has come clear through my journey of many lives is that if You Lord makes me imperfect, subhuman, that is my lot. I was wrong in loving something that my soul found beautiful and perfect. Even in my current journey that truth has been thrown at me from various religious beliefs. I am still in the eyes of this world sub human, born as a homosexual is abnormal; even through I had no say in it. I have a hard time understanding my lot. Even through you made me come back as a damaged good to teach me, my place and the error of my way, I still looked and found love. All theses days I believed it was humans who made laws and rules to break this world, your creation. Now I feel you are just as guilty, your traits of anger and superiority are all portrayed well in your followers. Yet I am a helpless imperfect piece of your creation. Where ever I looked for love you gave me pain. Do you in your infinite wisdom punish the bee for stealing the nectar of your perfect blossoms? Then why do you claim to be the beginning and ending of love, does unselfish love always end in pain. You have destroyed every temple of love I built in my heart. What kind of sick game are you playing? Subhuman as I am, I never want a tear to shed from one being. Where is your Godliness? Who is more like God, if you even exist? I am sure you do my Lord. I have never questioned or looked for evidence of your presence. I did not need any explanation for your existence. I never even searched for them. I do know for those who do not believe in your existence no evidence is enough. We, your creation give more credit to your god like qualities than it needs. At this moment my heart is full of pain for my first family, theses women who have been locked out of there home, the city of monkeys. Do you really feel it is fair to punish them for the mistake of a young sub human male? Punish me you did. What, for falling in love with perfection. Does not imperfection need love to make it feel complete and perfect? Is not that the purpose of creating perfect beings, so we who are imperfect can at least taste a bit of perfection in their love? You punished me to wonder as an imperfect being, a low caste woman, a slave, an uncivilized boy, even as a horse seeking perfection, every time I tasted it, excruciating pain followed. Please Great Creator, do not fate the same punishment again, make me a rock, so that I will bear the weight and blows of nature and who ever treads on me, but will not feel the pain in my heart. Now I am far away from my home waiting to journey in to the unknown to pay for my past crime, of seducing your son. I do realize that I used under hand ways to taste his perfection. You have to keep in mind great creator; I was a sub human, half ape and half human. You did not teach me the ways of your world. I lived by the jungle law, to love without reservation. To day I am standing on this rock, every thing stripped to walk into darkness. No God to guide me but ten sub human women, who do not even want me to see their faces. Tonight I will prove to you that although we were created in this form we are more powerful than you, my lord. All my lives I have knelt to show you respect and my devotion. I have lowered myself, my heart's desires, my wants and needs to do what I felt you would want. Starting tonight I will not kneel or lap water like a dog I will stand tall and demand you respect me as a worrier. This is the command you gave your chosen leader Gideon as he choose his 300 warriors. I have no fear but just the determination to correct my error so my family these ten beings can return to their homes and be reunited with their loved ones. Many great men have argued with you at your ways of dealing with us; let me chalk my name with them. Jacob, Job to name a few. I am not seeking answers oh! Great one, I am going to prove that my love for another man, even though he feels I am sub human is greater than your divine one. Tonight I am claiming any being with the spark of love in their soul is equal to you." Kumar felt a certain peace and anger fill him, and he noticed a tiny ray of light creeping through the rocky walls of the tall cliff.

Chapter 20 ......

Rectifying your past karma...

Kumar slowly stood up and stepped towards the light on the cliff, he turned to look at his guides or gang who were sitting around him; they seem to have disappeared into thin air. Only their small lamps stayed there blinking like fallen stars. Alone again, Kumar thought to himself and started to walk towards the light, his ankle bell kept the music according to his moods, So Kumar decided to face what ever came with absolute determination. The little bell made music to meet his resolute feeling. As Kumar neared the cliff the opening grew wider and he could see the cave deep within. Kumar crept into the cave and started to move towards the center of the cave. Pungent smell reached his nose, a sort of groaning noise faintly reached his ear, and strange shadows seem to flicker around him. Kumar then saw this hideous creature standing in the middle of the cave. Matted hair seem to cover very part of his deformed body. The creature's body was very muscular but muscles were hideously out of proportion and bulged like big boils all over its body. Kumar was stunned at the size of its penis and low hanging nuts. Teeth seem to cris cross all over its mouth like a wild hog, and saliva was pouring out of one side of its dirty mouth. Kumar hide behind the large rock to pull himself together, I seduced this being as a beautiful nymph but tonight I am going to seduce this creature in my original form. Kumar dug deep into his soul and searched for the deeply buried roots of his origin. Suddenly Kumar felt his form change, he became half human and half monkey. Pulling all his inner courage Kumar got close to the creature, it roared and planted both its strong hands on Kumar's shoulders and pushed him down to the floor. Kumar moved his ankle and the bell sounded a song of surrender. The beast seemed to be mesmerized and froze. Kumar bent and moved his tail and exposed his ass to the creature and tormented it with shaking his brown tight ass. The creature leaped and pushed Kumar to the ground. Kumar's eyes fell on the beast's penis and nuts. Kumar reached with hand and tugs the sac of the beast's nuts, squeezing it with all his might. Kumar was surprised at the strength of his monkey claws and how tight they squeezed the creature's nuts. The beast groaned. Its uncut penis shot erect, almost knocked Kumar off balance. Kumar without releasing his hold used his other hand to untie his leather head band and tied a knot as tight as he could around the beast's nuts. This seem to make the beast relax his hold, pushing its hands and wrapping his long tail on the creatures legs, Kumar jumped on the beast and knocked it flat on the ground. Kumar then straddled the beast and guided it hard baton like penis into his ass. Kumar, with all his might squeeze his splinter muscles and knotted the animal's penis into his body. Kumar kept moving his ankle to keep the music flow. The music sounded like an opera piece where the heroine was finally surrendering her body and soul to her lover. While gyrating his body, Kumar slowly untied the loin cloth which was pushed aside and covered the beast's eyes. Kumar very quietly unlocked Sita's Thali and wrapped it around both their heads. The beast pushed his wile looking tongue out, Kumar opened his mouth wide and sucked the tongue in and held it at its root with his teeth. The breast moaned and fought for his breath, all the while grinding it's groin deep into Kumar's ass. Kumar slowly removed the loin cloth blind fold and pried opened the beast's eyes. Kumar looked deep into the blood shot crusty eyes to search for its soul, just like Luxman had done to him. There in the deepest dark part of the beast's heart, Kumar saw a young frightened boy lying in a fetus position sobbing. Kumar's heart was filled with compassion, and he crept down through the slim and stench and carried the boy into the open. As

Kumar was climbing up, with this beautiful frightened boy into the light, Kumar noticed that Sita's thali had changed into a golden snake and coiled around both the beast and Kumar. As he reached the light, the beast little by little disappeared and there was Kumar's first love Luxman exploding his seaman into Kumar's ass. Both were completely made one. After hours of passionate love making, both collapsed on each other, the golden snake had twisted around them and kept them as one body. Kumar looked deep into Luxman's green eyes, while he looked deep into Kumar's brown eyes. Both only saw light, a torch of never ending love.

Chapter 21 ......

Journey home

Suddenly the cave was filled with bright light, the cave now looked like a king's bed chamber, and still wrapped in each others embrace Kumar noticed his guides, the ten women standing on one side, with their faces uncovered. They resembled Kumar's monkey face. They were expecting some thing to take place. Their garments glittered and shone. They kept chanting a soft tune that seems to calm both men. Suddenly the cave opened and flew in Rama and Sita

Kumar gazed at Sita's regal face. Her long black hair now seemed to be intermingled with grey, and flowed down to her knees. Her eyes were full of sadness yet she smiled and touched one of the seven heads of the golden snake. Like her thali had seven beetle leaves as pendants, each seemed to have transformed into seven heads of this golden serpent. Two heads bit into both men's first chakra the third eye. Two heads bit into their heart chakra and two into their kundalini or sex chakra. This awakens the sexual energy that lay dormant in the living. As Sita touched the one loose head the snake unwrapped it self, and became her thali. This released both men, and they stood up. Luxman greeted his brother and sister in law Sita by bowing at their feet. Kumar folded his hands with the normal greeting "Namaste". The women brought long robes and wrapped each man. Then a vision of bright light entered the chambers, everyone was blinded by the brightness and fell on their knees. "Welcome Lord of all creation, Lord Brahma" whispered Sita. There was stillness then a loud voice like thunder rang out, almost deafening every one.

"Well done my servant Kumar, you have freed my boy Luxman, and I have lifted the curse, your companions can find their way to the home, the city of monkeys, I will honor the old contract and your people will walk the earth and bring peace and joy where ever it is needed. As for you, sub human and imperfect form I will make you perfect and provide a home in my city, the city of the gods.

Kumar slowly raised and looked passed the opening on the chamber to spy on glittering domes of the city of monkeys. Kumar cleared his throat and in a voice soft and filled with fear said, "Sir, Lord of all creations, I thank you humbly with my whole being for your kindness, but with due respect and fear I am going to turn down your offer, my Lord. I have roamed this world for many lives. You in your infinite wisdom made me roam this earth for many years, many life times to learn the follies of my youthful sin. Falling in love with your perfect creation. I was made homeless, friendless and ridicule among those I lived. Even my immediate family turned against me, to sacrifice to the good of the so called society. I had wept to you and all the gods of compassion. You all remained silent. The only people who followed me day and night, through hell and heaven were my sub human family, theses ten women, who was punished just for being of my blood. They paid for my mistake yet they stood by me, even when I was at death's door they pulled me back. With due respect my Lord; you gods are just as petty as the humans who made on the higher chain of evolution. Lord Rama, you could not find love in your heart to understand the misfortune that fell on your loyal wife. You wanted more proof the thali, a gold chain. We sub humans found it for you. Goddess Sita, you walked away from you divine love and spent all theses years alone with a heavy heart. You my lady did not return to your family of Gods but lived as a hermit among us. My sweet Lord Luxman, I fell in love with your perfection as a god and man. I loved every cell of your existence, I lived on your breath, and found joy in your shadow, yet you only saw my imperfection hidden deep in my soul. I saw your imperfection as an ugly beast, yet searched and brought to light your true beauty. That lord in my heart is the true trait of gods. So my great creator I beg you to let me return to my home, my father's city, the city of monkeys and live with sub humans who accept my imperfection and yet love me. In your city of Gods I will be still imperfect and never be at peace". Time seemed to stand still, utter stillness seem to fill the room. Then Brahman spoke in a gentle voice, "As you wish my boy" and all the Gods slowly floated away. Kumar looked deeply into Luxman's green eyes for the last time. Kumar thought to himself even god's can have hearts that brakes. The ten women moved closer to Kumar, hugged him and grinned. Kumar finally felt he belonged and home was just a step away. All of them ran towards their home, the city of monkeys.

About the Author ......

Theivandran

The author Theivandran was born in Sri Lanka and migrated to the USA in the early seventies to complete his higher education. Newton finished his high school education in Sri Lanka under the British system, completed his under graduate work in India, and his masters in the USA. While living in India he studied the Indian classics Ramayana and the Hindu thought. In the USA he explored the Christian thought. He taught high school math for 36 years in the USA, around the east and west coast cities. He has travelled extensive around most of the world. In the mid eighties he was diagnosed with Aids and is a long term survivor. The discrimination against homosexuals in this country promoted him to weave this story. He is writing under his maternal family name-Theivandran (gift of Gods).